Dedication
To all those that refuse to whistle after dark.

CRYPTID CARL CHRONICLES

BOOK 1

HOLLOW KING

WAYLON GRAVES

This is a work of fiction. Names, characters, businesses, places, events, and incidents are either the product of the author's imagination or used fictitiously. Any resemblance to actual persons, living or dead, or actual events is purely coincidental.

First Edition

ISBN: 979-8-9993470-6-0

Design by William Buffington
Cover by William Buffington

For information, contact:
CryptidCarl.com
WaylonGraves.com

Printed in the United States of America

Acknowledgments
This book would not exist without my family.
Special thanks to my wife for driving me just crazy
enough to chase a dream, and to my son for
being my wellspring of inspiration.

PART 1:
UPON POWDERED WINGS

Chapter 1
A Town Light on the Living

It's been a month since the sightings began. No one thought much of it at first. Folks around here are steeped in old stories, tales whispered over fence posts, passed down over weak coffee and strong whiskey. In a town like this, heavy with graves and light on the living, everyone's seen something strange when the fog rolls in.

The place itself is old. Stone, carved out by a stream that once washed rebellion's blood into the Potomac. It cuts through the heart of town like a scar that never stopped bleeding. The past here is too heavy to let go. Storefronts stand shuttered, and the churches are long emptied of prayer. Only Mick's bar has life left in it, and even there, the ghosts outnumber the regulars. So when a drunk starts rambling most folks roll their eyes, until now.

At first, it was small things. A shape too big to be a bird slipping past the edge of your vision. A rogue wind curling down the alleys after dusk. Red eyes glowing from the steeple of the old Episcopal Church on Halloween night watching like some wicked star. Still, folks tucked their coats tighter and chalked it up to nerves, to the season, to old wives' tales.

Then Donna, who's been slinging eggs and coffee at the diner longer than most have been breathing, wrecked her car out by the cornfields. Some said deer. Others said something darker came out of the rows, teeth flashing and eyes burning.

By mid-November, the town's luck finally broke. A group of them saw it, plain and full-on this time. The story goes, that they ran from their picnic as the thing chased them to their soft-top convertible, speeding off with the top down and terror clutching their throats. Now the town's riled up like it hasn't been in years. They're sharpening old tools, dusting off shotguns, muttering prayers they haven't used in decades. A monster, they say. A curse come home.

Me? Looks to me like it just spoiled a bit of fooling around and left a couple of farm boys aching. Funny how quick fear can turn a backwoods town into a powder keg. But that's why I'm here. I clean up messes that don't belong to me, so I can keep what does.

Chapter 2
Secrets Over Scrapple

Donna's Diner is dingy and worn thin, like everything else in this town. No one's bothered keeping up appearances. An out of order sign rests across the soda fountain. The only warmth left in the place clings to a wall of faded, yellowing newspaper clippings— proud headlines from years gone by, kids long since grown and moved away.

I stand beside the crooked little sign telling me to wait to be seated. No staff in sight, just a couple locals hunched in the back booth, heads low. I grimace but stay put. Gotta make a good impression.

Then Donna clatters out of the kitchen, weathered, humorless, carrying two plates of greasy breakfast slop. She gives me a once-over and hollers, "You dinin' with us or what?"

I point to the sign. She rolls her eyes.

"Sit where you like."

I slide into a narrow booth, laying my rucksack down beside me like it might break if I'm not careful.

She stomps over, pot already in hand.

"Whatcha want?"

"Coffee."

Without a word, she tops off a chipped mug with thin, watery black.

"Anything else?"

A soft whimper rises from the sack. I press a hand to it, firm but casual.

"Yeah, scrapple... Bacon and eggs, too."

She huffs. "You got it. Comin' right up."

And just like that, she's gone, the kitchen door swinging shut behind her. When she returns, the plates clatter onto the table, and she tops off my mug with more of the black swill they call coffee. Before she can vanish back into the kitchen, I catch her.

"I heard you had some car trouble a couple weeks back," I say, casual.

She squints.

"What, you an insurance adjuster?"

"Nothin' like that, ma'am. Folks've been talkin'. Thought I'd get it from the horse's mouth, is all."

My hand drifts to the rucksack, easing it open just enough to slip in a chunk of scrapple. A soft, wet sniffle comes from inside, faint but sharp in the quiet. Donna's eyes flick to the sack, but she says nothing.

She snorts.

"People called me crazy until those kids saw it. Told me I hit a deer. But no deer ever rear-ended me."

"Rear-ended?" I raise a brow.

"Smashed the whole back end of my car in. Totaled it, mechanic said. Swore it looked like a bus plowed me."

"That's rough. You hurt?"

"Nah, not really. Skin's thin as paper at my age, bruises come easy. Nothin' worth fretting about."

Another faint sound, a sort of pitiful gurgle, rises from the sack as I feed it another scrap. I glance up. "Anything go missing from the car?"

Donna scoffs.

"Yeah, the whole damn rear end."

Before I can push further, one of the locals in the back calls out without turning around. Voice like gravel.

"She don't tell half the story, stranger."

I turn just enough to clock him in the corner of my eye. Older, eyes set deep under a heavy brow, nursing a life long hangover. Donna exhales sharp through her nose.

"Ignore him. Talks more than he listens."

"Well, why don't we have any pop in here then, Donna?" he grumbles, raising his glass.

"Nobody wants to hear it, Isaiah."

I lean toward him, masking the edge in my voice.

"What do you mean, friend?"

"That thing," he says, voice dropping to a conspiratorial rasp, "drank all the pop."

Donna rolls her eyes, but it's forced.

She addresses me instead, "I was stocking up for the breakfast rush. After the wreck, every damn BIB was gone."

"BIB?" I ask.

"Bag-in-Box syrups. Soda pop concentrate," she explains, deadpan. "Sugar water without the water."

The sack shifts again, pitiful and soft.. I place a steadying hand on it.

Donna narrows her eyes, suspicion creeping past the tiredness. "You sure ask a lot of questions."

I give her a crooked grin. "Curious by nature."

She huffs and disappears back into the kitchen, leaving me with Isaiah's stare and the quiet whimpering from the seat beside me.

To Isaiah, I ask, "You know where I'd find Roger and Linda?"

Chapter 3
Beer and Braggarts

Respectable men don't spend their mornings in dive bars, or so I've been told. Before noon, it's only the hopeless and the aimless, men who've run out of reasons to pretend otherwise. Mick's is packed with them. Old-timers slouched in cracked vinyl booths, bellies pushing against the limits of their poly-cotton blends. Faces slack. Eyes dim. Waiting out the clock with warm beer and cold memories.

At the bar, Roger holds court, crooked grin in full bloom, a liar's smirk carved deep into his face. He's spinning tales, loud and wild, each one more absurd than the last. The old men lap it up, offering him whiskey like pilgrims at a shrine, desperate for one more taste of excitement, even if it's secondhand and half-true.

I step up to the bar beside the boy, planting my elbows while he leans back on his own like he owns the joint. He's soaking in the attention, grinning wide, drunk on the adoration of old, spent men trying to remember what it felt like to matter.

The bartender gives me a nod. "What'll it be?"

"Water. And fresh nuts, if you've got 'em."

"Water?" Roger bellows. He's already deep in his cups, eyes glassy and cheeks flushed, riding the high of his own story. "You won't drink with us?" he slurs, his gaze sliding toward the scar that splits down the side of my face. His smirk falters slightly, just for a moment.

I glance at him sideways. "Bit early for me, friend. Heard you saw somethin' out in the woods. Where was that, again?"

He puffs up. "Me and my buddy were out at Morgan's Grotto, neckin' on our girls when—"

I cut him off. "They see it too?"

He stammers. "Who?"

"The girls."

"Oh, yeah. 'Course they did!" he says too fast. "We all saw it. Thing flew outta the trees like a damn nightmare—red eyes, all black, wings big as a pickup!"

"What'd it do?" I ask.

Roger puffs up, all bravado and booze. "I'll tel you what it did. Attacked us. Chased us all the way to town!"

"You must've been pissin' yourself," I mutter. "So what'd you do?"

Before he can answer, the bartender slides a cloudy glass of water and a bowl of bar nuts my way. I dump the nuts straight into my sack, zip it closed, and take a sip.

The water tastes like pool chemicals and pennies. I slide it back across the bar.

"This from the springs?" I ask, confused.

"Nah," the bartender says, wiping down a glass. "Tap comes outta the river."

I blink. "You got seven springs feedin' that damned stream—and y'all drink outta the river?"

He shrugs. "I didn't plan the damned town."

Chlorine masks the taste of old corroded lead lined pipes. Whatever I was about to ask Roger gets lost somewhere in the back of my throat. Roger notices my attention slip and flares up, drunk and offended.

"Hey! You wanna hear this or not?"

"I'm listenin'," I say, still swishing chlorine on my tongue. "Get to it. What'd you do when the demon came for ya?"

Roger puffs up like a rooster in church. "I grabbed my girl, threw her over my shoulder, and ran to my convertible! Tossed her in, slid across the hood like in the movies. Got it in gear just as it came down on us. Slammed the gas, tore outta there."

He throws his hand in the air, nearly knocking over a half-empty shot glass. "But it was right overhead—right over us—with these BIG RED GLOWING EYES!"

He pauses for dramatic effect. I sip again at my glass and wince. I slide it away.

"I was doin' over ninety when it hit us. Whole damn car spun out, damn near flipped—crashed into the town sign."

"And then what happened?"

"Whatcha mean?"

"The dreaded black demon with the glowing red eyes," I say slowly, "flies ninety miles an hour, slams into your car... and then what? It just... lets you go?"

Roger fumbles. "I-it disappeared. Vanished. Into the night."

"So you're tellin' me this monster's whole plan was to make you piss your britches and scratch up your fender before headin' on its merry way?"

"I—I didn't—"

"Alright then," I cut in, calm as can be. "Anything missin' from the car?"

"Huh?"

"Did it take anything? Snacks? Drinks? Your virginity?"

Roger bolts upright, face flushing.

"You sonofa—"

"Well?" I ask, deadpan. "Did it, or didn't it?"

"No... nuthin'. I mean, we left a cooler back at the park, I guess."

"Your girl, Linda, right? Works the Dollar Store down the hill?"

His eyes go sharp. "Why you askin' about L—"

"Appreciate your time."

I casually walk out of the bar into the cool autumn morning light without a goodbye.

Chapter 4
A Dollar for Your Fear

The dollar store is empty, stale, and soulless. Black and yellow signs scream about discounts on junk—cheap, gaudy products made by slaves an ocean away. They wrecked a million lives here for their high ideals, only to trade them for the spoils of someone else's misery. All of it destined for landfills, choking on plastic and dust. But I'm a shopper and shoppers shop.

I grab a plastic bottle of 'spring water' from the grimy fridge and drift toward the unmanned checkout. A small, cracked bell sits on the counter like an insult. I slap it and the clatter echoes hollow across the aisles. The rucksack at my side stirs. A soft, wet whimper. I press a steady hand over it. "Easy now," I murmur. The sack shivers faintly beneath my touch, unsettled but obedient.

Nobody comes, but I notice movement in the back. Linda's there, headphones on, stocking shelves with vibrant-colored boxes, lost in the drudgery. She's young but worn down, that hollow-eyed look of someone who's already accepted the dead-end. The sack shifts again, tense. I draw a quiet breath and slip down the aisle, each step careful and deliberate.

I slip into her line of sight. The faint buzz of pop music bleeds from the cheap headphones clamped over her ears. I offer a polite smile, raising the bottle and gesturing to it.

She pulls the headphones down around her neck, blinking herself out of whatever daze she was in.

"Sorry to bother you," I say with a smile. "Just wanted to pay for my drink."

A flicker of embarrassment crosses her face, softening the deadened demeanor. Reflexive kindness surfaces, that old small-town habit. She mumbles an apology and we head together toward the checkout.

"Say," I venture, voice casual, "aren't you Roger's girl? Linda, right?"

Her brow knits. "Do I know you?"

"Nope, never had the pleasure. Rog and I go way back." I lie smoothly.

"Name's Carl. Real nice to finally meet you."

She exhales, a soft note of wariness beneath the small-town politeness. "Yeah... sure."

I press on. "Heard you had a bit of excitement the other night. Whole town's in a tizzy, but I can't get a straight word out of anyone."

That does it. Her face stiffens, shoulders drawing in a touch. Her eyes sharpen. "You ain't the first come 'round snoopin' in my business."

My eyebrow raises to this news.

"I doubt you're with that gossip-column hack," she adds, voice low but steady. "And you sure as shit, ain't with those suits."

The sack at my side lets out a faint, anxious sniffle. I ignore it, but Linda's eyes flick briefly to the movement.

"What do you want?" she presses, a thin edge of steel beneath the question.

I offer the faintest of smiles. "I'm just a curious fella."

She rings up the water, eyes on me the whole time.

"Right... cash or card?"

I don't move. "I just want to know what you saw. And what you were doing before you saw it. That's all."

She notices I'm not reaching for my wallet, and neither of us pretends this is a transaction anymore. The silence hums louder than the old lights overhead.

Finally, she exhales. "Fine. We were out at the park, havin' a 'picnic'. Saw this big black thing—demon-lookin', with red eyes and wings. It flew outta the trees and came at us."

"Attacked you, how? Anyone hurt?"

She shifts on her feet. "Flew at us. Fast. We bolted to the car and tore outta there."

"Did it follow you?"

A beat. She narrows her eyes. "...Are you with the law?"

"Linda, I don't care if you were getting high or tangled up in the woods. I'm not here to tell anyone's business—I just need the truth."

She hesitates, then sighs. "Rog made up the part about it chasing us. Truth is, he wrecked his car outside town and needed a story."

I nod. "So, underage drinking, foolin' around, and didn't want the sheriff sniffin' out booze in a wrecked car. That about right?"

"Yeah," she mutters, embarrassed but relieved to get it out.

"Okay. But this demon—real or bullshit?"

Her eyes harden again. "It's real. I know what I saw."

"What were you drinking?"

"Nothing crazy."

"Whiskey? Gin? Vodka? What?"

She huffs. "Rog and Steve were makin' Dew Drivers."

"Dew Drivers?"

"Mountain Dew and vodka."

I let it sit between us for a beat, sharp and cloying, like the drink itself. The rucksack squirms faintly at my side, restless. I press a steady hand over it.

"Thank you for your time, Miss," I say, smooth and measured.

I slip the water bottle into my coat pocket and turn for the door. As I near the exit, her voice follows—quieter this time, touched with hesitation.

"You... you didn't pay for that."

Chapter 5
Deals with Eels

I pull into the cracked lot of Town Hall in my rusted-out red Ford pickup. The engine coughs wheezes and squeals as I park. In the rear window, my gun rack cradles my trusty old boom stick—barrel dull, but reliable. In the bed, a blue nylon tarp stretches over something bulky, tied down tight with fraying rope. The corners flap a little in the wind.

I kill the engine and climb out, boots hitting the gravel with a crunch. I take a breath, square my shoulders, and smooth down my thick black hoodie. It's stained in places, salt and something else crusted along the hem. I hitch up my jeans, tug them into place like it matters. I rub at the stubble on my jaw, then slick my greasy hair back with the flat of my hand. Respectable. Presentable. I'm a professional, after all. The driver's side door doesn't close right, so I slam it. Twice. That's our cue. Showtime.

Town Hall looks like it used to matter. Long time ago. The brick facade still holds a kind of dignity, but the inside tells the real story. Fluorescent lights buzz overhead, too bright and too cold. The floor tiles are cracked, curling at the corners. Rooms have been split up with warped sheets of plywood, nailed together in a rush—cheap, makeshift, and permanent in that way temporary things always seem to be.

I step through the door and make for the front desk. The receptionist clocks me immediately, tight-lipped and regretting her life choices. She's clacking away at a keyboard with the aggressive rhythm of someone already having a bad day.

Can't say I blame her. I probably smell like a combination of wet dog and skunk. Maybe I should've taken that dip in the river. But I'm here now, and there's no turning back.

"Afternoon, ma'am," I say with a polite nod. "Name's Carl, Cryptid Carl. I've got an urgent matter I need to bring to the mayor's attention."

Her brow arches like she's just been asked to babysit a raccoon. "Do you have an appointment... sir?"

"No, ma'am," I admit, calm and steady. "But it concerns the recent trouble in town. It's a matter of life and death, I'm sure of it."

That gets a reaction, not from her, but from the young blonde sitting nearby in the waiting area. She perks up, her local newspaper forgotten in her lap, eyes flicking to me with sudden curiosity.

The receptionist doesn't flinch. "If it's so urgent, I'd suggest you speak with the sheriff. He's down the hall, first door on the left."

"No, ma'am," I say, gentler this time. "This needs the big man. Directly."

She sighs, tapping her pen hard against the desk. "Well, you'll have to wait your turn. As you can see, you're not the only one here. I can put you on the list."

I nod, masking my frustration with a tired smile.

"Yes, ma'am. Of course."

Just then, the rucksack at my feet lets out a low, snuffling whimper, followed by the faint rustle of rummaging from inside.

The receptionist narrows her eyes. "Sir, animals aren't allowed in the building."

I flash a grin. "He's my emotional support animal."

Then I step back and ease into a chair, the rucksack settling at my feet with a soft grunt. The girl across the room keeps watching me, eyes wide with curiosity, like she's just caught sight of her story.

I took the seat across from the blonde, closer to the mayor's door. She's pretty, sharp around the edges, polished in that way people get when they've read too many articles about success. Not from around here. The posture, the tailored coat, the faint whiff of expensive lotion. Some self-entitled Northern Virginian, I'd bet. Probably here to poke around in things that don't concern her, but what could a girl like that want in a place like this? I wonder. Is she the gossip-column hack? If so, who are the suits then?

My leg bounces with impatience. I take a breath, deep and deliberate, filling my lungs until my ribs ache. I hold it there, long enough to feel the pressure swell, then let it out slow. Quiet. The tension bleeds off, just a little. I can't afford to let this take too long. Minutes pass. The mayor's office door opens with a click, and out he comes, all handshakes and wide smiles. Schmoozing with two local businessmen, all pressed flannel and forced laughter. Backroom dealing, I think. Good. He's not cucked by the town council. That's good for us.

He slaps shoulders and shares some parting wisdom, and as he turns to the room, "Well, who's next?"

Before the receptionist can open her mouth, I'm already on my feet. "That'd be me, sir. Carl. Cryptid Carl. It's a pleasure." I reach out and shake his hand firm but warm, already steering him back toward the office door with a practiced ease, like this is a meeting we've both known was coming.

He doesn't protest, caught off guard by my confidence, maybe, or just too polite to push back. The receptionist's eyes narrow, but she doesn't say a word.

The blonde is suddenly on her feet behind us. "Hey!" she shouts, just as I pull the door shut in her face.

Inside, the mayor adjusts his jacket, mildly flustered. I cut straight to it. "Sir, I'm sure you're well aware of the attack that just happened to four of your young townsfolk, are you not?"

He nods, giving a politician's smile. "Why yes, I'm well aware. Well aware of the situation. The sheriff's department has been notified and they're acting accordingly. Now—what does that have to do with you?"

I meet his gaze. "Sir, do you know what you're dealing with?"

He scoffs. "Just a bunch of hubaloo."

I step closer. "It wasn't that many years ago this creature appeared in another town. Same strange sightings. Same hysteria. It all ended with a bridge collapse on Christmas."

His face stiffens. He mutters under his breath, barely audible: "The Mothman?"

I nod. "You've got a couple bridges heading over the Potomac... and Christmas ain't that far off."

"That's insanity," he says, shaking his head. "There's no such thing as... Mothman."

"Even if it is all bull roar," I press, "you've got dozens of drunk men riled up, ready to 'defend' their town from a monster. You really think none of 'em are gonna get someone killed?"

He frowns, caught between disbelief and dawning concern. "What... what is it you're even proposing? Who are you?"

Before I can answer, the door flies open.

"Hello, Mr. Mayor," the blonde says, breathless but determined. "My name is Beatrix Beaumont. I'm a student journalist from—"

The mayor raises a hand sharply. "Miss! This is incredibly rude. You've interrupted a private meeting."

She jabs a finger toward me. "He's the one that barged in!"

I turn to her with a calm smile. "Miss, you should've made an appointment like the rest of us."

She huffs, face flushed, biting back what's clearly a scream.

I turn back to the mayor without missing a beat.

I straighten up, meeting the mayor's skeptical gaze with the calm of a man who's done this before. "Sir, my name's Carl. I hunt the world's most unique and mysterious animals, creatures most folks write off as myth or madness. Cryptids." He opens his mouth, but I keep going. "When trouble arises, real trouble, towns call on me to handle the problem. Quiet, professional like" I pace a little, slow and steady, like I'm laying out a deal over a campfire. "Some towns want the issue gone without a word. Keep the boat from rocking. Let folks get back to their lives like nothin' ever happened." I glance toward the window. "Others... well, others see opportunity. A mystery, a legend—it's fuel for stories, for tourism. Think Roswell. Loch Ness." I turn back to him. "This town's already talking. You've got something here, like it or not. This could be your chance to either make it disappear... or put it on the map."

The mayor narrows his eyes. "What exactly are you suggesting?"

I smile, easy but deliberate. "What would it do for this town if the Mothman ended up stuffed and posed in your historic museum?"

He blinks, stunned by the directness of it. Somewhere between disbelief and curiosity. "How do I know this isn't some kind of scam?"

"That's a fair question," I say, calm and measured. "You strike me as a smart man, Mr. Mayor. Careful. Practical. I respect that."

The rucksack beside my chair shifts faintly, just a small rustle and a soft thump. No one notices.

"I'm not asking you to take my word for anything," I continue. "I'm asking you to step outside and take a look at what I've brought with me. It'll speak for itself."

Beatrix scoffs under her breath, then says, "You really think there's anything you can show him that will convince him that you're some monster hunter?"

I don't look at her. I don't have to.

"Mr. Mayor," I say, rising to my feet, "if you'll follow me."

He hesitates, weighing something in silence, then nods. "All right."

I open the office door and step out into the lobby. The receptionist raises her eyebrows, but says nothing.

Beatrix is already following the mayor out. "You've got to be kidding. You're seriously going with him?"

The mayor gives her a firm glance. "Miss Beaumont, I'll hear what the man has to say."

She huffs and follows anyway, arms crossed tight against her chest, heels clicking behind us with righteous fury.

I lead the way out the front doors, down the steps, and into the late afternoon light. The wind's picked up a bit—enough to flap the edge of the blue tarp stretched over the truck bed.

The mayor stops a few paces short of the tailgate.

I turn to him, calm and composed. "You wanted proof."

I lead the mayor around to the back of my beat-up old truck. The tailgate drops with a metallic thud that echoes across the parking lot. Beatrix trails behind, peppering me with pointed remarks like I'm some backwoods villain, but I keep my focus squarely on the mayor.

"No, Mr. Mayor," I say, holding a hand out. "I'd like you to steel yourself. What I'm about to show you may shock and amaze."

I grab the tarp and throw it back in one motion, revealing the hulking, hairy mass beneath. The creature fills the truck bed—its limbs limp, its massive hands curled like fallen branches. Its fur is thick, coarse, and a strange pale blond.

The mayor recoils slightly, then gasps.

"My god... a Bigfoot! You bagged Bigfoot?"

I shake my head, gently correcting. "Strictly speakin', this ain't a Bigfoot. This here's a Yaya. Also known as a Yellowtop, on account of the color."

Beatrix is frozen—staring with wide, tear-filled eyes. Her face is twisted in something between disbelief and heartbreak. A single tear slides down each cheek, but she says nothing.

The mayor, meanwhile, is lit up with excitement. "This town... this town would attract people from everywhere if we had Bigfoot and Mothman mounted in the museum!"

"Well now," I say with a smile, "like I said, this here's a Yaya. But yes, it's a rare one."

"Yes, yes, you're very knowledgeable," the mayor says, waving his hands. "How much do you want for it?"

"Sir," I reply, "this creature ain't for sale. I've got to deliver him—"

"I'll pay double," he cuts in.

I pause, then grin. "Sir, that sounds like a deal to me. But I need payment up front. Taxidermy don't come cheap." I lean in just a touch. "Now, you see, I only take money for work already done. Don't want noone sayin' I don't deliver on my promises, so I ain't chargin' ya a cent fer Mothman. Not 'til he's hangin' on yer wall."

The mayor nods slowly, hanging on every word.

"But," I continue, "I do need the funds now for the Yaya. My taxidermist's the only one I'd trust with a creature this... unique. If I don't get him preserved soon, he's gonna start to stink... well, worse."

I extend a hand, firm and ready. "So, you help me cover that cost and I'll turn my full attention to that winged devil terrorizin' yer town. We have a deal?"

We work out the costs with brisk efficiency. The mayor, still riding the high of discovery, scribbles figures onto a notepad and makes a call. Within the hour, he hands me a cashier's check with a proud little flourish. I take it straight to the local bank and exchange it for cash; clean and untraceable, just how I like it.

Beatrix, of course, is not pleased. She trails behind us the entire way like a storm cloud with good posture, tears cutting sharp tracks down her cheeks. After the mayor parts ways, practically whistling as he walks off to tell his buddies about the museum's future crown jewel, she rounds on me.

Her eyes burn. "You murdered him," she spits. "That creature was alone in the world. And you just... killed him. For money! Like it meant nothing."

I don't answer. I've heard every variation of that sermon. Still, there's something in her voice—raw, pleading—that gives me pause.

She steps closer to the truck bed, brushing past me. Slowly, like she's approaching a casket, she places her hand on the creature's thick arm, then slides her fingers down until they find its enormous hand, leathery and heavy, curled like a child's.

She gasps and freezes like a doe in high beams.

"It's warm," she whispers.

A moment later, the creature's massive, barrel-shaped chest rises. Then falls. Then rises again. From deep in its throat comes a low, guttural snore, thick with phlegm and fatigue. Beatrix jerks her hand back, covering her mouth. I stare for a beat, jaw tightening.

"Unbelievable," I mutter, full of annoyance, throwing the tarp back over the creature in one swift motion.

I slam the tailgate shut with a crash and turn to the girl.

"Time for us to get going now." I hustle around the front of the truck, throw open the door, and slide into the driver's seat. I barely get the keys in the ignition when—slam—the passenger door swings shut.

Beatrix is beside me, eyes blazing. "You're not going anywhere until I get some answers."

I groan, crank the key. The truck growls to life. I throw it into reverse.

She grips the doorframe. "Hey! I'm serious—!"

But I've already backed out and shifted into drive. Gravel kicks up behind us as we shoot out of the lot, past Town Hall, and out beyond the welcome sign. By the time she fumbles with her seatbelt, we're a mile past the last streetlight.

Chapter 6
Few Can Refuse

"You can't just take me! This is kidnapping!"

I don't respond. Not right away, just keep driving until I spot a dusty old convenience store with flickering lights and a broken ice machine out front. I pull in and throw the truck into park.

From behind the seat, I pull out a knotted plastic sack, then dig around until I find what I'm looking for: a pair of stained, torn, and foul-smelling denim overalls. I lift up the tarp covering the truck bed and toss them in.

"Time to put away that wrinkly scrote, ya damned useless fool."

The tarp lurches. Then undulates. Underneath, something moves slow and purposeful. A moment later, the tarp flings back. The massive, blond-furred Yaya sits upright, now dressed in the rank old overalls, wearing a lopsided grin that stretches nearly ear to ear. He scratches his gut and peers into the cab.

"Who's the stowaway?" he asks, voice deep and full of amusement.

Beatrix screams.

"Some sort of admirer," I mutter, tossing a thumb her way. "Didn't you hear her callin' you a beautiful and unique creature? Or were you too busy snorin'? You almost blew the whole operation."

Yaya stretches his massive arms and yawns like he's waking up from a vacation. "We get paid? Where's my cut?"

Beatrix just stares, mouth parted, eyes locked on the enormous yellow haired, talking ape-man now crouched in the back of the truck. The blood drains from her face, then rushes back in a hot, confused flood.

"Hello, my dear," Yaya says with a sly grin, offering a slight bow. "What's your name?"

"B-Beatrix," she croaks.

"A pleasure to make your acquaintance," he says with mock elegance. "Are you joining our little escapade?"

"Wh—what do you mea—"

He waves her off and turns to me. "Her cut's comin' outta your share, not mine."

"Blow it out your ass," I reply, pulling a folded wad of bills from my coat and slapping it into his palm. "She ain't comin'."

He counts the cash with a grin, then stuffs it into the front pocket of his overalls. Beatrix stands there, fists clenched, her whole body locking up as the situation finally breaks her brain. Then she explodes.

"What is going on here!?"

"My dear girl," Yaya says with a dramatic flourish, "there's no reason for such an outburst. You may call me, Yaya Yellowtop, and this here is my pet, Carl."

"Fuck off," I mutter.

The rucksack sits open on the tailgate between us. It rustles suddenly. Then, rising slowly like a cursed jack-in-the-box, an unfathomably hideous head emerges from the bag. Amphibious. Pig-like. Dog-like. Wet and glistening. The creature blinks at Beatrix, then curls what might be a smile across its face.

"Squonk," the creature croaks happily.

Beatrix yelps—a sharp, breathless sound—and drops like a stone. Yaya, unfazed, catches her with one dirty bare foot and lifts her gently with his broad and hairy arms. The squonk, horrified by her reaction, begins to sob like a dog hit by a car. It buries its face deep into my sweatshirt, its tears soaking through almost instantly. I sigh and gently pat its back, the way you'd calm a panicked child. Yaya hoists Beatrix up with one arm and dumps her into the passenger seat of the truck.

"So what's her deal?" he asks.

I don't look up. "Far as I can tell, she's some prissy college girl tryin' to write a paper on the strange goings-on 'round here. She doesn't care much for me hunting big game, it seems."

Yaya chuckles, low and rumbling. "Well, she's got spirit."

"She ain't comin'," I repeat flatly.

He nods, stretching his arms. "It's almost dark. We don't got a lotta time to get this done."

"She ain't gettin' paid."

"Well, I sure as shit wasn't gonna pay her." He snorts. "Why'd we stop here anyway? Whatcha need?"

As I clear out the bed of the truck and swing the winch arm out from the side of the frame with a creak, I hum low and gravelly: "Them that refuse it are few... I'll hush up my mug if you'll fill up my jug... with that good ol'—"

"Yeah, yeah, I got it, pal," Yaya grumbles. "Jesus, your voice sounds like a raccoon caught in a chimney."

Beatrix startles awake at the soft knock on the passenger window.

"Wakey wakey, princess," Yaya coos through the glass, voice gentle like he's waking a child. "We got work to do."

Her eyes snap open and she immediately recoils.

"What the hell was that!?" she shrieks, the memory of the squonk's grotesque visage still burning in her mind.

"Now, now," Yaya says, unbothered. "That's not a very kind way to talk about our friend here. He's been real put out by your little outburst."

"Wha...?"

"No worries!" Yaya chirps, flashing a grin. "We can forgive your deeply rooted speciest behavior if you help us out a bit."

"Speciest?" she repeats, blinking hard.

"Keep up, darling," he says, gesturing toward the convenience store behind them. "I need you to pop in and grab some soda. The green stuff."

"What? I don't have any money. Wait, you just got a wad of cash! Why don't you go?" She meets Yaya's eyes and finally notices his flat features, the wide simian jaw, the too-deep eyes. Her voice softens. "Right, but I still don't have any money."

I shout from the truck bed, "Rich girls got credit cards!"while standing with one boot on the wheel well, carefully coiling the cable from the winch with practiced hands.

From the cab, Beatrix shouts, "Why should I help either of you?"

Yaya, finally running out of patience, responds flatly without even turning around. "Look, we thought you wanted to help. Thought you cared 'bout the plight of that poor beast," he pauses just long enough to twist the knife,"didn't think you were the type to watch an endangered species get repo'd." He pauses, then gestures to the road with a lazy thumb. "If you're not gonna help, hit the bricks."

The message is clear. She's getting out of the truck one way or another. Yaya trudges toward the convenience store, arms swinging low and wide like they're weighed down by the indignity of it all. He mutters as he goes, "This is beneath me. I should be basking in a hot spring, reading my book in peace... not fetching sugar water for some overgrown butterfly."

"Wait!" Beatrix blurts, scrambling out of the truck and hurrying after him. They enter the convenience store together, the doorbell chime cutting the awkward silence like a blade.

Done with the initial setup, I sit quietly on the trailer hitch, stroking the dark, damp canvas of the rucksack. The squonk, my Squonk, inside begins to take shape again, its form shifting softly as it coos a quiet, pathetic sound meant only for me. These hunts are rarely clean. They're always dangerous. Anything could happen. Nothing could happen. That's the problem.

I close my eyes and take a breath, slow and deep. I center myself. Each breath I draw and release brings me closer to a sense of peace. In that peace, Squonk grows and solidifies underneath my hand. The remaining light filtering through my shuddered eyelids, fill my senses with an all consuming red. Some say, meditation is a way to slow down the world, stop it even, maybe enter 'nother.

Across the parking lot, the bell above the convenience store jingles. Yaya and Beatrix emerge, their arms overflowing with sloshing 2-liters of green soda pop.

"We cleaned out the store!" Yaya shouts triumphantly, the bottles clinking together as he lumbers toward the truck.

"I still don't understand what all this is for," Beatrix mutters, struggling under the awkward weight.

Together, they dump the sugary cargo into the bed with a cascade of plastic thuds.

I eye the girl, then glances to Yaya. "She make good?"

"Yep," Yaya says easily, dusting his hands. "Didn't even blink swipin' Daddy's credit card. Real team player."

For the first time, I meet her eyes, really meet them.

"Why exactly did I have to use my parents' credit card for all this? It's meant for emergencies." she asks, arms crossed, expression tight with suspicion.

She's kind of pretty in this light. The sun's low now, soft gold spilling across her features. That rich-girl thing she's got going on doesn't look so bad in the glow. Shit.

"Fuck... It's golden hour. We gotta move."

Yaya's already climbing into the driver's seat. I hand him the rucksack, careful and quick. Squonk rustles softly inside. Yaya takes it without a word and places it gently in the center of the bench seat like it's made of glass.

"We're going to Morgan's Grotto," I say.

"Got it," Yaya replies, tossing his paperback onto the dashboard and firing up the engine.

Behind me, Beatrix throws up her hands.

"Oh, come on! Are you going to talk to me or what!?"

I point toward the truck. "You comin' or what? Get in."

The urgency is rising in my chest like a drumbeat. We're going to miss our shot. I brace myself in the truck bed, crouched and steady, just as Yaya slams his foot on the gas. The engine roars to life, gravel spits from the tires, and we're off.

Chapter 7
Bubbling Dread

Morgan's Grotto would be green and verdant in spring, surrounded by lush woods and soft hills. But it's autumn now. The leaves are gone. The color's drained out of the land like old blood, and the trees jut from the soil twisted and bare, curled like desperate, searching tendrils.

The sinking sun stretches long, dark shadows across the brittle grass.

"We gotta get this done quickly," I say. "Lady, grab the netting behind the seat."

Beatrix fumbles around, then reaches behind her seat and hauls out an awkward, heavy duffel bag, its canvas sides scuffed and stained.

"Little help?" she asks Yaya, struggling with the duffel.

He glances at her over the top of his wrinkled paperback, expression flat. "I don't do manual labor." Then disappears back into the pages like she never asked.

Beatrix slings the heavy strap over her shoulder with a frustrated sigh and trudges awkwardly out into the meadow where I've already dragged the cable across the leaf-littered ground. Yaya smirks behind his book, clearly amused by the sight of his young protégé working alongside the girl.

"Good," I say under my breath as she arrives, dropping the bag with a dull thud. I unzip it and begin pulling out the bundled netting, unfolding it carefully across the brittle leaves. "Grab your end," I tell her.

She nods and takes it. We walk in opposite directions, unfurling the massive net into a wide circle across the clearing.

"So... we're hunting Mothman with a giant butterfly net?" she asks, skeptical, but no longer mocking.

"Trappin', but yeah. That's about the size of it."

"And the pop... is the bait?"

"Yep."

There's a pause. Then her voice softens. "You're not going to kill it, right?"

I pause, sighing long, deciding how much to give her.

"So, there's huntin', and there's trappin'," I say, "and I don't know how to hunt a bird without blowin' it outta the sky." I glance at her, just long enough. "I got a place. Where it won't hurt nobody, and nobody'll hurt it."

"How? Where?" she presses, eyes narrowing.

I don't answer. Instead, I nod toward the net. "Cover it up with leaves."

She hesitates, watching me for a beat longer, but then crouches and starts brushing fallen foliage over the nylon mesh. I gather the bottles of soda from the truck bed and carry them out to the center of the trap, placing them carefully in a clustered ring labels facing out, like that matters, caps twisted just loose enough to fizz. Bright green bait in the middle of dead brown leaves.

Chapter 8
Unspooled Yarn

It's dark now. I sit in the bed of the truck, still and watchful. Squonk curls in my lap like a sad, wet cat, his weight warm against me. I stroke the back of his misshapen head absently, eyes locked on the trap. The cluster of soda bottles glimmers faintly in the inky field, barely visible.

Up front, the girl sits beside the great, fat ape. Yaya flips the pages of his crumpled old paperback, eyes squinting in the glow of a dim dome light. After a while, Beatrix glances him up and down, then turns to the sliding rear window, cracking it open.

"So... how'd you get into monster hunting?" she whispers toward me.

"We're not monsters," Yaya replies flatly, his nose still buried in the book.

"Quiet," I growl.

Yaya snorts, louder now, not even looking up. "A bunch o' people squawkin' never scared it off before. Why should it start now?"

A sharp flash of anger rises in me, but I can't fault the logic. If anything, it might be drawn to the sound of chattering fools. I let out a long, heavy sigh.

"Fine."

"So... how'd this all get started?" she asks again, softer this time.

I sit with the question for a moment, chewing on it.

Before I can answer, Yaya blurts out, "Oh, we've been doin' this for years now. We got bills to pay. Well, he does, anyway." He flips a page with his thick fingers, still not looking up.

"How many more... creatures have you... helped?" she continues her interrogation.

"Some," I say, keeping it short, not wanting to brag or sound incompetent, either.

Yaya pipes up again without missing a beat. "Chicks dig scars, tell her 'bout the time you got your face half ripped off.'"

Startled, she turns, her eyes drawn to the long, jagged scar winding its way down the left side of my face. She quickly looks away, uncomfortable.

I glance her way, then back toward the tree line. "You ever hear of the ghost hounds?"

She hesitates. "Ghosts..." Her eyes flick to Yaya, then back to me. "Did that... to you?"

"Well," I say with a dry laugh, "if they weren't ghosts then, they sure as shit are now."

She goes quiet. The dome light gives just enough glow to catch the edge of her face, but I can't read what's behind it. I shift in my seat.

"Yeah, well... we tracked the ghost hounds down to the Cheat—"

"The Cheat?" she interrupts.

"It's a river," Yaya says. "And a lake, sort of."

"Anyway," I go on, "these hounds had been causin' all kinds of trouble. Livestock turned up gutted, shredded. Whole county was spooked."

"And that's when you got caught in the middle of a scrap between a pack of ghost hounds and the Snarly Yow," Yaya cuts in, grinning like he's just delivered the punchline.

I shoot him a look. "You tellin' it or am I?"

He shrugs, all innocence. "Just helpin' move it along."

I lean back, the scar on my face tight in the cold. "There we were. Me and my busted shotgun. On one side, snarlin' glowing' see-thru hounds with eyes like lanterns. Other side, the Yow, the biggest black dog you've ever seen. Lookin' mean and hungry."

"And you survived," Beatrix says, almost like a question.

Yaya huffs a laugh. "His face didn't."

I tap the scar with two fingers. "Chicks dig it."

Beatrix snorts. "Keep tellin' yourself that."

After a beat, she starts up again, "Why do you do this, then?" she asks, "If it's so dangerous?"

"She's got a point," Yaya chimes in, still lounging in the cab. "We've got the money. We could just high-tail it back to the mountain and call it a day."

"I'm staying," I say flatly. "You wanna sit this one out, be my guest. Walk back."

Another pause.

"Do I need to tell the girl how I found you?" I add, without looking up.

"You wouldn't dare," Yaya mutters, finally lowering the book and turning toward the window.

"Please," she says, "we're all friends here right? Call me Bex."

"Well, Bex," I begin, "I met this stinking' tub of lard treed by a bunch of hound dogs up in the Sods. Bear hunters and their dogs thought they bagged themselves a real prize."

"The indignity... I was in quite the predicament," Yaya admits, lifting his chin like he's telling it first.

"That's horrid," Bex starts, "but there's no reason—"

"Quiet!" I bark, eyes snapping to the tree line.

The air shifts. Something is coming. The night has taken on an odd stillness. Then I hear the faint heavy thump of wings. Slow. Rhythmic. Too large for any bird I know. The slow, melodic beating turns into a sudden maelstrom. Wind tears through the trees.

Then it's there. A massive black shape drops from the dark above, landing square atop the trap. Its wings stretch wide and unnatural. Twin red eyes glow like coals in the night, casting just enough light to make the bottles of soda shimmer beneath it.

I crank the winch hard. The net snaps closed with a hiss and a whip of cable. The beast thrashes once, then lifts—hauled upward into the air, trapped, limbs tangled in mesh. It dangles from the thick limb of an old sugar maple like some grim trophy.

"Smooth as butter," I say, a rare smile creeping in. More for the girl than myself. But in my head, I know better. It never goes smooth.

Yaya slowly backs the truck beneath the old maple as I crank the winch, reeling the creature in like the catch of the day. The netted beast sways just above the bed—massive, still, and black against the inky midnight sky.

Squonk approaches first. Timid. Careful.

"Squonk... squonk... SQUONK... ssqqquoonk," he murmurs, voice low and wet and oddly soothing. A strange lullaby.

I climb into the bed and reach out slowly, placing my hand on the creature's dark body. Light. Calm. Just enough to show we're not a threat. A light dust of powder clings to my fingers. The beast stirs.

Within the folds of the net, it shifts. Great wings rustle and turn, just enough to reveal those glowing red eyes. They fix on me. Alien and intelligent.

"Hey, pal," I say gently. "Sorry for all the trouble, but we're gonna take you somewhere—"

The great black mass groans, deep and unnatural, against the netting. Then it breaks. With a sudden snap, the mesh tears loose. Massive wings unfurl with a thunderous whump, and in a single beat, the creature launches into the sky entangled in shreds of netting.

I don't even have time to shout. My arm, tangled in the cable, jerks with violent force. The world lurches as my boots leave the truck bed and I'm pulled up, screaming through the air like a rag doll behind a jet engine.

Chapter 9
A Fall from Grace

Searing pain shoots through my shoulder. My arm nearly torn from its socket as I'm whipped higher into the dark, the earth dropping away beneath me. I claw at the netting with my free hand, finding purchase near the creature's feathered mane. Gritting my teeth, I pull myself up, inch by inch, until I'm straddling its back. Wind whips at my face as the world a blur beneath us. We tear through the night sky, zagging and zigging under the stars, the Mothman bucking and twisting like a bronco from another world.

Below us, I catch a glimpse of the truck rumbling down an old service trail—Yaya at the wheel, swerving like hell. Bex is in the truck bed now, clutching a few green soda bottles to her chest like her life depends on it. I dig in. Gripping the torn netting like reins, I jerk hard to the right and down, twisting the tattered fabric tight around my fists.

The creature lets out a shrieking cry, metallic and ancient, and spirals into a sharp dive. We smash through a tree. Branches crack and explode around us, and I'm flung from the creature's back. Instinct kicks in as I lunge and catch the edge of the torn netting, fingers screaming as they grip rope and fabric. My other hand scrambles, finds another hold, and clamps down.

We're lower now. I feel it. The air is heavier. The wind bites harder. Headlights slice through the dark ahead of me, blinding, glaring through the trees as I flail beneath the beast like a ragged banner.

I'm dead weight. A human anchor. A heavy, swinging pendulum that drags at the creature's flight, slowing it, making its movements lopsided and sluggish. The headlights rush forward, flooding everything in white. I see the truck bed below me. It's close, but not close enough.

Still too high. I glance up. There, near my hand, is the cinch cable tangled in the net. The knot, one chance. I let go with one hand and reach. This is it. I grab the cinch line and hold it firm, then let go of the net.

I drop faster than expected. Further than expected, slamming into the truck bed with a sickening thud and bounce up and over. I'm about to roll clear off the side when small fast hands grab me. Fingers lock around my jacket and pull me hard against the wheel well, holding me in place.

Before I can even register what's happening, I shove the end of the cinch cable into a waiting carabiner, already hooked to a mount in the truck bed. There's a shout. Tires screech. The truck brakes hard, fishtailing across the rough dirt road. The line yanks tight.

Like a hooked fish, the creature is ripped from the sky. My momentum, and the sudden stop, drags it down into an emergency landing, crumpling the roof of the truck with a metallic slam.

The black figure towers overhead, seething, a nightmare made flesh. Its wings curled, chest heaving and red eyes piercing the night. Beside me, Bex's breath is hitching, too stunned to scream. Half my body's numb. The other half, I wish was. I wrap one arm around her and pull her close, shielding her with what's left of me. I brace myself for the wild assault of a wounded animal.

"Let's all calm down a sec and talk this out over some pop," Yaya calls cheerfully from the cab, like we aren't seconds from being torn apart. He reaches out with one long, powerful arm and gently lifts Squonk onto the roof of the truck, holding a plastic bottle in his squishy arms like an offering.

This is where the little aspic shines. Soothing, softening, making peace where none should exist. The stories say he's the ugliest thing in creation. They say when he cries, he becomes water, a puddle, but that isn't quite right. He's always water and the ugliness we see in him is just the reflection of the ugliness in ourselves. His tears aren't for himself, but for the pity he carries for the world.

And it works. The creature above us shifts. Its wings relax. Its burning red eyes flicker and dim slightly in the dark. Then, slowly, it leans down and begins to drink from the bottle. Its long, curled tongue unwraps and plunges into the plastic like a straw in a sacred ritual.

I let out a breath and lower myself onto the edge of the truck bed. I let the pain rush in, sharp and all-consuming. Throbbing ribs, aching limbs. My whole body's one big, pulsing bruise. I take a deep breath, hand pressed to my side, and look up at the creature.

"Sorry we got off on the wrong foot," I tell him. "We're not here to hurt you." It watches me, still and silent. "You've got a lot of people riled up... from one end of the state to the other. We just wanna take you someplace safe. We got a place for ya. Real nice one. You won't be alone there."

The creature doesn't move. Doesn't blink.

I sigh, unsure if any of it means a damn thing.

"Hell," I add, "we'll throw in a case of pop once a week to keep ya happy. What you say?"

Yaya chimes in from the driver's seat, voice deadpan. "That's comin' from your end, NOT mine."

Squonk lets out a soft, tentative squonk. His little voice full of gentle encouragement. The kind of sound that says it's okay now. Both Squonk and the creature turn to look at me.

"Squonk," Squonk says.

I toss the Mothman another bottle and gesture toward the back of the truck. "Get under the tarp," I tell him, voice low. "It'll be morning before long, and we've got a long drive ahead."

Chapter 10
Where Monsters Lie

We rumble our way through graveyards and the skeletal remains of homes, barns and churches, hollow shells of dreams long abandoned. Symbols of hope rot along the roadside, surrendered to time. As we wind deeper between farms and forests, the ruins grow fewer but more desolate, as if we are entering a place few dare to tread. The Appalachian mountains, worn low by eons, sag into rolling decay, all except our destination. Ahead, a jagged stone spine juts from the earth, defiant and untouched by time and crowned by a dark lenticular cloud churning with a restrained violence. Bex stirs in the middle seat, eyes fluttering open. She's nestled between a snoring ape and a softly grunting gelatinous Squonk, curled in her lap like a weeping furnace. We're climbing past the Dutch community and rolling through the long abandoned company town, before I take the opportunity.

"Wanna thank you," I say just above the road noise, "for what you did out there. You kept a level head. You really—"

"Yeah, I really saved your ass," she mutters, still half-asleep.

I smirk. We round a curve, and the landscape opens up below. Mist rises off the trees, soft light painting the edges of the world.

"Where are we?" she asks rubbing sleep from her eyes.

"Home."

The place where all this started. I park the truck in a clearing near my beat up trailer. The gaping maw of the mine belches a heavy plume of black smoke that coils into the sky just beyond the bend. The chickens are already scratching at the ground for gravel and grubs. I kill the engine and ease out of the cab, sore and stiff. The chickens rush me.

"Move off! Harold, get your women under control." I shout to the speckled cockerel.

I slam the truck door, jolting Yaya awake with a grunt.

"I need you to release our new friend," I tell the surly simian.

He yawns, long and dramatic. "Clearly, I have to do everything around here…"

He lumbers out of the truck as the others gather behind the tailgate. Yaya pulls the ties free. The great beast rises beneath the tarp, then throws it off with a single motion. Wings unfurl wide and catch the rising sun. Morning light cascades through the stained-glass shimmer of its wings, casting swirling rainbow patterns across our faces.

Bex gasps, clutching my arm instinctively. I wince, but not too much. Her warmth presses into me, and for a moment, I don't feel the pain.

"Think I'll name you, Mortimer. Mortimer Moth has a good ring to it." I say. Mortimer drops an empty bottle at my feet. I grin and toss a fresh one into the air above our heads. With a gust of wind, he's airborne with the bottle cradled in his arms soaring toward the tree line before disappearing into the woods without a sound.

"And that's why we do what we do, young lady," Yaya says with a smile, watching her still clinging to me. He smirks, clearly pleased with himself.

I glance at her, the warmth of her hand still on my arm, the light still dancing on her face.

I tell her, "Welcome to Storm Mountain."

PART 2:
THE PHANTOM
OF FLATWOODS

Chapter 11
Salted Wounds

The chickens and rabbits are fed. I'm spent. I plop down into my weathered, sun-faded lawn chair by the fire pit and let my eyes close.

"So... I have an issue," Bex announces to my shut eyelids.

Here we go. Bring one woman into the mix and suddenly I can't get a moment's peace. "...Yeah?" I grumble, making it clear I don't care.

Something tugs at the swollen, twisted thing that used to be my arm. It's mottled in shades of bruised plum and overripe kiwi, the skin stretched tight and shiny in places, pocked with deep red and yellow splotches. It hangs limp from my shoulder, half-hidden in the folds of my sweatshirt like I've been trying to pretend it's not there.

"What the hell are you doing?" I snap, jerking slightly.

"What's it look like?" she fires back, pulling my arm into her lap. She starts wrapping it with an Ace bandage, like she's been planning this since sunrise.

"We have a first aid kit?" I think, vaguely impressed.

Now that she has my attention, she dives in. "I left my car back in that town. You know, when you kidnapped me."

I begin, dry as ever, "I didn't kidnap you. You jumped into my tr—"

"The parking spot has a two-hour limit," she cuts in.

I sigh. "...And you got no way off this mountain."

She finishes the wrap, secures it with a little metal clip, and presses it gently back into my lap. I dig into my back pocket, pull out my wallet, and peel off a few crumpled hundreds. I press them into her hand without looking.

"You ain't our prisoner. And you earned your cut."

She stares at the money.

"Use it to pay for the ticket," I mutter before passing out.

Chapter 12
In the Eye

I wake to the sight of a dingy, water-stained ceiling and faded wallpaper peeling at the corners. Poorly constructed columns of musty and yellowed books hold up the ceiling above me. An ancient mattress sags beneath me, flat as a dead possum and twice as lumpy. Yaya must've hauled me into the trailer sometime after I passed out. Beside me, something warm and heavy is pressed against my side. Good ol' Snarly. I stumble out of the trailer, squinting into the morning sun. Everything hurts in that dull, familiar way, the kind of pain that means I'm still alive. The morning light stabs straight through my skull.

I shift my weight onto the massive, invisible hellhound, using her like a crutch. No one sees her, but by the light of the moon. Her shaggy and impossibly large frame holds me up and moves in step with me. Out by the rabbit hutches, Bex is holding one of the kits. She cradles it close, stroking its fur with a silly, tender smile. Her face lit up with childlike enthusiasm.

"Well," I sigh, eyeing the little scene, "this doesn't bode well for our meat production."

The smell on the wind is damn near intoxicating; grease, smoke and whatever Yaya managed to scrape together for breakfast. Without a word, my support shifts beneath me. Solid and silent, for a moment it feels as if I'm wrestling a bison, before I relax and let her guide me toward the fire pit, with my hand resting on air. Yaya's hunched over beside the cast iron, sausages frying while he fiddles with that contraption of his. Its some sort of radio he's been cobbling together over the last few years.

By the time I limp my way over and sink into my old weathered aluminum lawn chair, the sausages are burned black on one side and raw on the other.

Snarly huffs into the pan, the scent too much for even a spectral beast to resist. She inches closer, ready to gobble up the sizzling mess.

"Get back, ya mangy mutt!" Yaya barks, waving away the hot breath of my invisible companion. He snatches one sausage with his enormous fingers and flings it far into the trees.

A dog's yowl echoes faintly, followed by a sudden gust of wind that rattles the fire pit and leaves us in peace.

"You're teachin' her bad habits," I mutter.

"Yeah, yeah," Yaya chuckles, not looking up. "My bad habit is teaching my pets bad habits. I spoil you all so."

I roll my eyes at him and start nudging the remaining sausages around the pan, trying to find the least-charred parts. They hiss and spit like they're offended by the effort.

Yaya returns his attention to the contraption, turning a few knobs with those massive fingers of his. It crackles, then comes to life. It emits a blaring and unnerving wall of static that makes my teeth ache.

He twists the dial, and the noise rips through channels—ghosts of sound flickering in and out. First, the strained wail of church music, warbling and off-key. Then a tax relief ad. Something about "lifetime forgiveness."

Then it settles.

A flat, somber voice fills the clearing: a community news broadcast, slow and steady, reading out the names of the dead.

"You finally got that thing workin' proper?" I ask, eyeing the radio.

Bex finishes putting the rabbits away and joins us around the fire. She settles into the chair next to mine—closer than I'd expected. Maybe she's just cold. Or hungry. Maybe both. I take a quiet breath, slow and steady, trying to ignore the way her knee brushes mine.

She listens for a moment, then asks, "What exactly are we listening to?"

"It's the community obituaries, right now," I say.

She blinks. "Is that... normal around here?"

She wasn't really asking anyone in particular, but she glances my way when no one answers.

"Community stations read 'em out," I say with a shrug. "Not sure why we're listening to it," looking over at the ape.

Yaya says, "The other day I got a garbled report about something going on in Flatwoods."

I sigh, "What's Fanny up to now?"

Squonk slithers into my lap. I offer him a sausage, which he happily gnaws on, slow and content.

"No idea. When we get to town, keep an eye out for a discone antenna."

"A disco antenna?" I ask, blankly.

"Discone," he corrects.

"Who's Fanny?" Bex asks.

"Another... friend," I say, with some reluctance. "One who might need help, if she'll take any."

I dish her up a sausage and put on a smile that doesn't quite reach my eyes.

"I'm sure you want to get back to your life. I try not to make a habit of returning to towns I've already worked over—"

"You trying to get rid of me already?" she interrupts, half-mocking.

"I'll take you to your car," I say, more clipped than I mean to be. "You can decide what you want from there."

I hate myself for hoping.

"Are you kidding?" she says, eyes wide with fire. "I need to know about this place. I need to know about them."

She gestures toward Yaya, hunched over his contraption, and Squonk, who's still gnawing on a sausage like a depressed possum.

"You can't write about this place," I say, looking away. "I know you fancy yourself some kind of journo."

"I'm in school to become a writer," she says, bristling. "I was here to write about a town locked in fear and superstition, but this?" She shakes her head. "This story's too big. I have to write it."

"No one'll believe you."

"Then why are you worried?" she fires back, calm and sharp.

I rub my face with the one arm I've still got that works. The pain's still there. So is the headache.

She leans in, already pitching. "Look, you like money, right? Sell me the rights to your story!"

I blink. "What now?"

"We split the profits—fifty-fifty—off anything I publish. For perpetuity. Got it?"

Yaya glances up, chewing lazily. "That means for all time."

"I know what it means, you damned fool."

I look down at Squonk.

He pauses, sausage half-eaten, and stares back up at me like he's the only one here who truly understands the weight of eternity. I contemplate the offer.

"You can't tell people where we are," I say, voice low, resigned. "...and you can't use my name."

"Of course!" she squeals, and without warning, throws her arms around the ape. Yaya looks startled for half a second, then leans into it like it was his idea. I catch myself flushed, not from the pain, or the fire, but at the thought that she might be sticking around.

God help me.

Chapter 13
Coming Down

Rumbling down the mountain in my rusted heap, Bex comments on the old ruin of the company town. Most of the houses are collapsed. The ones still standing are sagging like drunks too stubborn to lie down. Only one structure remains mostly untouched—an old warehouse, weathered but intact, save for its roof.

When I was young, my folks never let me near the place. After they were gone, I kept my distance for different reasons. I didn't have anyone in my corner back then, and all I could afford in those days... was caution. Eventually, I gave into curiosity. Pried open the warehouse and stepped inside.

It was mostly rot, mold blooming like tumors across the walls, cockroaches darting from the shadows, mice where sacks of grain used to sit. The stench of time and forgotten purpose. But then I found the crates. Big ones. Government stamped. Faded but legible.

U.S. Ordnance – Dynamite – Surplus.

Wartime leftovers, stashed and abandoned. When I cracked them open, the red sticks looked cartoonish to my kid brain, like something out of Saturday morning television. They felt more like toys than tools. So I played.

I blew up stumps. Split boulders. Sent shockwaves down through the hollers just for the thrill of it. Would've tried fishing with it if there were any lakes worth the effort in this damned fold of the country.

Later, through stolen books from a shuttered library, I'd learn more. The dynamite was used to blast out mine shafts and when the coal wars kicked off... they were used for something darker. Some days, the bad days, I'd catch myself staring in the direction of that old crate. Thinking too hard and too long. Tired of my past of being tethered to this birthright of mine, like a dog on a rusted chain. Surviving when I never asked to. On those days... it's a good thing I stopped carrying matches.

Back down the mountain, in the ruin of a town that had been menaced by Mortimer just the day before, everything is still. It's as quiet as its cemeteries. The streets are nearly empty. And those few who remain out turn their heads as we pass, watching from porches, sidewalks, behind dusty windows. We rumble through in the rusting heap I call a truck. Their faces are blank. Unwavering. Like they're waiting for something else to fall from the sky.

"Something feels off," Bex says, her voice low, uneasy.

"Just the imaginings of a lady who had her world flipped upside down," I reply, keeping my eyes on the road. "We'll make it quick. Bank, post office, then we get you to town hall to pick up your car. Don't wanna linger. Then we scoot on over to Flatwoods, got it?"

She doesn't answer right away. Squonk gurgles softly in her lap, like a damp tea kettle trying to hum. "What are we doing at the bank?" she finally asks, watching the empty streets roll by.

Chapter 14
Gold for Wolves

"Gold for wolves," I tell her. "If they can't steal it one way, they'll find another. I pay a ransom each month to keep the brutes off my land. A tax lien, is what they call it."

"How much do you—? Wait, how long have you had the land? How'd you even get it?" She fumbles the words, like they're tripping over each other trying to get out.

"Family land," I say. "Always been. Ma and Da raised me there. My Da's Da ran the mine down the ridge. When they—passed, it took a while for anyone to notice. I was still a kid, tryin' to survive. Didn't know nothin' about taxes or lawyers." I shake my head. "They tried to take it from me, but now I pay Danegeld, to keep the invaders at bay."

She studies me. "So that's why you—?"

"Why I work the towns? Their councils, their leadership?" I nod. "Yeah. Figure it's best to pay the creeps with their own money."

She narrows her eyes. "That's not how that works."

"It's close enough," I say.

At the bank, I convert what's left of the wad into a cashier's check. Fill in my info, slide it into an envelope with the recipient's name scrawled across the front like a bad afterthought. I walk it to the curb and drop it into the blue mailbox.

"Let's get your car," I say, already walking. "I don't want to linger here."

I hand the truck keys to Yaya, "Get it back home." He grunts, already climbing in. As the truck pulls away, I watch my father's rifle disappear into the distance, shrinking with the tailgate. I pat the iron on my hip. Not exactly naked, but I feel the difference. Bex's vehicle turns out to be a Ford too, a small, green and shabby looking car. Looks to me like Yaya could sling it over his shoulder like a sack of potatoes. Didn't expect that from little Miss North Virginia.

"I'll drive," I tell her.

"Like hell you will," she snaps, sliding into the driver's seat before I can argue.

I get in beside her. The car sits low to the ground, way too low. I feel like I'm sitting on the road. It's disorienting.

"It's like a damn tin can," I mutter.

"What?" she says, not hearing me over the wind and road noise.

I glance around the cramped interior, then at her.

"Just figured a rich girl from north of Richmond would be drivin' somethin' else, is all."

She snorts. "I'm from Berkeley... California."

That surprises me.

"Dad moved us out east for a job at a defense contractor," she goes on. "I started school north of here, last year."

I nod slowly. "You're really gettin' around." Then I grin, sharp. "So, Daddy moved you from the land of peace protests to help blow 'em up?"

She gives me a sideways glare while I snigger.

Chapter 15
Sinners Under Steeples

We arrive in Flatwoods as the sun begins to sink. The town is empty. Still. Except for the church bells, blaring and echoing off the empty storefronts.

"Some kind of service is in session," her stating the obvious.

"Maybe it's a pancake dinner service. Could we be so lucky?" I ask trying to mask my excitement.

Bex and I slip in through the double doors, quiet as can be. The place is packed to the gills with everyone in their Sunday best. "Is it Sunday?" I wonder, vaguely. My sense of days' long gone to hell. The pastor stands at the pulpit, giving a sermon, or a speech, or whatever you call it when a man in cloth gets up in front of a crowd to tell them what to do, who to be, and to hell with you if you disagree.

There's something off about him. His smile's too wide. Too fixed. Inhuman, like one of those prosperity televangelists who sells salvation and snake oil in the same breath. I slump into the pew beside Bex. She sits straight, proper, listening like a good little schoolgirl. I sprawl, limp and half-gone, fiddling with the bandage on my arm, twisting the old wedding band on my middle finger, the one that used to belong to my father.

I must have drifted off, because suddenly an elbow jabs me hard in the ribs. I suck in a breath, barely biting back a curse.

"Was I snorin'?" I whisper.

Bex doesn't answer, her wide eyes stare at ne with pointed jabs, then points toward the pulpit. The pastor is talking about an angel. No, a phantom, he calls it. He speaks of it with reverence, calling it a sacred vessel, a being of truth. Says it holds knowledge that will bring them closer to ascension.

"What kind of church is this?" I whisper.

The pastor raises his arms, his grin splitting impossibly wide. He introduces someone new to the stage. Their guide to greatness. The doors behind the pulpit open. And he steps out.

Indrid Cold.

My ruined hand comes alive before I know it, snapping to my jacket pocket. The cold steel of the .357 Magnum finds my fingers like it's part of me. I'm on my feet in a breath. The blued frame clears the fabric—up, steady, aimed. Three shots explode from the short barrel, deafening in the cavernous church.

Boom.

Boom.

Boom.

Bex screams, her voice barely cutting through the ringing in my ears. "What are you doing!?"

The tall, pale man with the too-wide smile jerks as the bullets hit, then crumples against the podium like a rag doll. But there's no chaos. No gasps. No running. No one moves, except Bex. The rest of the congregation simply turns to face me. Slowly. Synchronously. Every single one of them grinning that same frozen rictus smile.

Bex sees it, really sees it, and starts to tremble. I'm likely to beat her to full-blown panic. I turn back to the pulpit. He's gone. My heart lurches. I grab Bex by the arm, pulling her with me toward the exit, my revolver sweeping across the room. My finger tightens on the trigger, looking for any trace of the body. Anything.

Creaking wood. Dozens of feet shuffle in unison. I spin, he's in front of me. Just there. Standing too close. The smile unchanged. The eyes, black and wrong.

"Hello, Carlisle," he says.

Two more explosions erupt from my revolver, straight into his chest. Then, click. Click. Useless now. The empty cylinder spins as the creaking crowd begins to shuffle toward us, slow and steady like they've done this before. I squeeze Bex's arm and shove her toward the doors. We bolt daisy-chained, pulling and pushing each other faster with every stride and reach the green tin can she calls a car.

"I'm driving." I shout. She tosses me the keys without a word. I catch them midair with a jingle and we slam into our seats. I wake the pitiful engine, stomp the accelerator, and we lurch forward, jumping the curb, tires screaming as we tear down the road.

From the back seat, my rucksack stirs. Squonk pops out, squonking with concern, his wrinkled face furrowed in alarm. His watery eyes plead for understanding I don't have time to give.

Bex is shaking. "What the hell was that!?" she yells, voice cracking with fear and fury. Too much noise. Too many voices. Too much.

"SHUT UP! SHUT UP! Just SHUT UP!" I bark, the sound bouncing off every inch of this thin metal box back into me, "We need to get to Fanny. Now."

Bex stares at me, angry and confused, but she doesn't push. She takes a breath and asks, "...Where's Fanny?"

I keep us barreling down a narrow, winding mountain road, twisting hard between cliffs and rock walls, the edge just feet from

our tires. No guardrails, simply a sheer drop into fog
and forest below. Headlights swing wildly with each turn
as I grip the wheel tighter.

Chapter 16
The Phantom's Cathedral

The trees cast long, inky shadows across our path. My flashlight cuts through them in thin slices, revealing the trail just a few steps at a time. Squonk clings to my back, quiet but tense. Bex follows close beside me, her boots crunching in the dead leaves.

"She's a temperamental, skittish bitch," I mutter. "If we spook her, we'll never get her."

"You've tried before?" Bex asks.

"Few years back," I say. "Kinda gave up on the idea."

There's a pause then, "Who was that back there? What were those people?"

I shake my head, eyes still scanning the woods.

"Don't... I don't know about the townsfolk," I admit, "but that guy, his name is Indrid Cold, the Smiling Man. There've been sightings of him all over the state for the last decade. No one's been able to pin him down. I don't know why, but they're after Fanny." I grip the flashlight tighter, "Well, that fucker can't have her."

We step into a clearing. A small mound rises from the earth like some ancient burial ground, covered in moss and crowned with stone.

I sigh. "We'll set up here."

Bex looks around. "What's the plan?"

"The flashlight'll attract her. Far as I can tell... she just wants her kin."

I shift the weight on my back, turning slightly to glance at the little glob of sadness clinging there.

"It's all up to you, buddy," I say softly, "you think you can talk her into coming with us?"

Squonk squonks soft and uncertain, full of trepidation.

"Yeah," I whisper, "I know."

Bex and I sit beside a natural windbreak in the stone, just a few feet of elevation, a miniature cliff against the eerily flat terrain at our backs. We wait in the dark, quiet, watching the mound. Squonk lies in the center, draped around the flashlight like putty. The beam stretches into the sky, dim and steady, casting pale light across the skeletal branches overhead.

My breathing's heavy and unfocused. I haven't seen that face in ten years, now I can't unsee it. That fucking grin. He didn't seem any older from that day. I reach into my shirt pocket, fingers curling around loose rounds. Feels like the right size. I squint toward the light, just enough glint to read it. .38 special. I sneer, irritated, but load them anyway.

He needs to die and I need to kill him. A soft hand rests on my leg. It pulls me back, back to the clearing, to the mound, to Squonk and the woman beside me. I take a deep breath, slow and steady, and click the cylinder closed. I squeeze her hand gently and slide the revolver back into my pocket. And then, something changes. The black ink of the forest begins to recede, washed away in color.

The trees shimmer. The light bends. A soft, iridescent glow spills across the clearing, like oil on water, like moonlight refracted through some unseen veil. A small smile tugs at my mouth.

"Ever seen a rainbow at night?" I ask her quietly.

She floats daintily over the ridge, larger than a man, smaller than a bear, lighter than air.

Her wide, round eyes glimmer in the dark. A long, narrow torso tapers into a bell-shaped skirt of lappets, flowing like silk in water. From them radiates a soft, prismatic glow shifting and refracting. Like an angelic jellyfish swimming through the sky.

"There's our girl, Fanny," I whisper to Bex.

"She's... beautiful," she breathes, full of awe.

Fanny lowers herself, gliding down toward the mound. She hovers, cautious, then dips her glowing form closer to Squonk. He squonks gently, then more urgently. A soft series of coos and watery clicks. She pulls back at first, startled. But then, slowly, she drifts toward him again, drawn in by his song.

Chapter 17
They Came a Crawlin'

They stay like that for a long while, maybe ten minutes, moving in delicate circles around one another, a dance of color and sound. Then, Squonk flashes the beam toward us. A quick flicker, their signal. It's time to introduce ourselves. Bex and I rise together, slow and steady, careful not to break the spell. But as soon as Fanny sees us, she shrills in alarm and shoots upward, wings pulsing in panic. Squonk freezes, the beam still locked on us. I don't look at him. I look up to the ridge behind me, where a glint of reflected light cuts across too many teeth grinning in the dark.

From the trees and soil, they emerge. A horde of townsfolk crawling from roots, stepping from shadows, closing in like a tide of rotted Sunday suits and glassy eyes. They throw nets over Fanny mid-ascent. She screams, high and otherworldly, thrashing as they drag her down. Her radiant glow stutters, fracturing across the trees like shattered stained glass.

We led them here. How? They made no sound. Not a single crunch of leaves, not a twig snapped. They must've crawled in slow as slugs, inch by inch, through the branches and brambles. I'm frozen in my own astonishment, just a second too long.

It drops from the ridge; Indrid Cold lands behind us like a shadow peeled from the sky. In a blink, he's twisted Bex's arm behind her back, his hand sliding across her throat, holding her like his own personal meat shield.

"I'm less than happy, with how many times you shot me this evening, Carlisle," he says, scolding me like we're family. My revolver is in my hand before I even think. But the flashlight begins to swing wildly, slicing light through the clearing in a violent, blinding strobe. I can't see Bex. Can't see him, then I hear it "squonk, squonk, squoooonk" building like a squeaky battle cry.

Squonk barrels toward us from the mound, fast and frantic like a fat show dog at full sprint with the flashlight clenched in his mouth. With a final burst, he leaps an elegant, wet arc and spits the long black cylinder straight into my hand before vanishing with a splash into my open rucksack.

I have eyes again, find Bex. I scan the clearing, vision sharpening. Indrid drags her toward the mound, his hand still locked around her arm like a shackle. The horde is pulling Fanny in too, nets taut, her glow flickering wild across the trees in psychedelic bursts of fear and pain.

"Oh Carlisle, come join us," Indrid calls. His voice is warm, almost giddy, "I want to show you something special this evening."

I've shot Indrid five times—five—in the chest with a .357 Magnum. I want my rifle. I want Snarly. Hell, I'd settle for that great yellow haired buffoon, but right now all I got are four rounds of .38 Special, and they probably won't do a damn thing. I have a police-issue flashlight that doubles as a club and a folding knife. What the hell can I do? I got nothing. He just got up, over and over, like nothing happened. There's maybe twenty of them now, maybe more, all wearing that same stupid grin.

If they're anything like him...

What can I do?

"Oh, Carlisle!" he calls again, cheery.

"Come on down! I really don't want you to miss this."

I take a deep and slow breath to fill my chest and gut. Then hold it long enough to feel my pulse slow. I let it go until I'm empty and my mind is still. I step forward casual, loud, crunching through sticks and leaves without apology.

The scene is set: Indrid with Bex at his side like a prize. A dozen grinning husks pinning Fanny to the ground with nets, her glow pulsing in rhythm with her panic. Squonk has my back, and I've got enough hate in me to raise hell. I approach the grin-cutter and slide my rucksack off onto one shoulder.

"Carlisle Boone Cold," he drawls, grin wide as sin, "you don't call; you don't write; such a disappointment."

"What do you want, old man?" I ask, keeping my voice cool and even. That Cheshire grin, those black eyes, still as smug as the day he emerged from the dragon's throat.

"It appears we share a common interest, dear boy," he says tone lilting like a man offering cigars at a wake.

"I think we can help each other."

"Oh? And how's that?" I ask.

"I want to offer you a position in the family business, you see," his smile never faltering.

"Doubt you'd set foot in a mine again. What business did ya start up exactly?" I ask, voice level as I sidestep through the leaves. "Seems to put a smile on every face I see."

My eyes never leave Indrid. Bex is still locked in his grip, his hand curled tight across her neck, holding her half-suspended between us. She's struggling to breathe, lips parted, eyes darting. We are surrounded by darkness, except for the pulsing glow of the angel, Fanny. Her body bound in nets, wings strobing in panicked bursts of color that flicker wildly across the trees. I shift another step to the side. Indrid mirrors me. Step for step. I angle myself so that Fanny's strobing light is at my back, casting me in silhouette, shadow-wrapped and unreadable. Let him squint into the chaos.

He laughs a low, bubbling sound like someone choking on honey. Then he opens his shirt. Inside isn't flesh. It's hollow. A cavernous ribcage, dark and gleaming, pulsing faintly with an unnatural heat. Nestled inside, dozens of eggs. Pearlescent. Veined. Shifting. One is hatching. The slick head of something insect-like pushes through the membrane. A hellish cicada the size of a rat. It twitches and clicks as it emerges, glossy wings still folded tight.

"Grandson," Indrid purrs, "I want to put a smile on every face. That's why I need your help. It seems we share a passion for hunting rare specimens like these."

His grin sharpens.

"Tell me... what do you know about the Thunderbird?"

I don't blink.

"The Ford Thunderbird was introduced in 1955," I deadpan.

Indrid squeezes Bex's neck harder. Her eyes widen as psychedelic tears cascade down her cheeks, shimmering like oil slicks in the strobe of Fanny's panic.

"Okay okay!," I say, hands raised. "I know it! I'll tell you everything I know, just let them go. You have my word."

He holds my gaze for a long, unbearable moment, then releases her. I catch Bex mid fall as she collapses forward gasping and fighting for air.

"If you want the bird, release the Phantom now," I demand. The creeps hesitate, then, one by one, release their grip on the net. Fanny begins to rise, wings flaring out in a burst of color that sets the woods ablaze with light. I slide the rucksack onto Bex's shoulders, Squonk still tucked inside. Then, with everything I've got, I grab her by the belt and fling her behind me. She screams, once, before Fanny catches her—scooping them both into the sky in a streak of radiant light, vanishing across the stars like a comet.

Chapter 18
Heir to the Hollow King

Three out of four ain't bad. Seventy-five percent is a C, right? Never really made it to school, got this son of a bitch to thank for that, don't I? But I hear, C's get degrees. I swallow the lump in my throat and turn to face Indrid.

"I only know two things 'bout the Thunderbird," I say summoning my best Bruce Campbell impression, "Jack and shit, and Jack left town."

Before I can move, his hand is around my throat. He lifts me like I weigh nothing.

"There's no need to be so crass, Carlisle," he purrs, the smile never slipping. "Even if you don't know where it is, you know others who might." He leans closer. "Soon, I'll know them all too."

From his chest, the hatched insect crawls, slick jointed legs clicking on bone and cartilage as it scuttles up the arm that holds me suspended in the air. I jerk, thrash, and kick, anything to break free, as the thing crawls closer to my face.

"You always were troublesome. Never gave your parent's a moments rest, did you? There's no need to fight," Indrid coos. "Don't you want to see them again? Join us."

I sputter through clenched teeth, "You killed them, you fuck."

A shot cracks the night. Indrid's arm jerks back in a spray of black ichor, and the insect explodes in a wet hiss of chitin and fluid.

Thank you, .38. I'll never call you 'special' again. I drop like a stone and hit the ground rolling.

Then I run. Into the dark. Blind. Choking on breath. No idea where I'm going, just the vague hope that I'm headed the same way Fanny flew. I trip over roots. Slam into trees. Crash through brush and stumble over rocks and ruts. Every step is pain. My body's wet, freezing, torn open on thorns and bark. Just a slab of meat flung through the woods, but I don't stop. I hit a cliff face at full speed, gasping out a cry as the stone slams into me.

Cold, jagged rock towers into the void above. I don't think. I climb. Fingers numb. Muscles screaming. Every movement is a fresh torture. I claw upward like a dying man crawling out of his own grave. I don't know how long it takes, but eventually, somehow, I drag myself through a narrow crack in the rock, a cave. I slide inside, roll and fall into the void slamming into cold rock and sliding through a narrow passage.

The dark... is unmovable. Inside, it's nothing but stone and silence. Solid, ancient, indifferent. No light. Not a glimmer. I'm blind in here, but also, finally, invisible. No footsteps behind me. No glowing eyes. No teeth. I sit, trembling. Breathing hard. Hyperventilating, really.

I force my hands over my limbs, checking for breaks, tears, pain I haven't noticed yet. Everything hurts. Everything's wet. Everything's cold. But nothing's missing. That's something. Slowly, slowly, my breath evens out. The panic slips its claws loose, just a bit. In this quiet, suffocating dark, I reassess.

No light.
No Squonk.
No Bex.
No weapons.
No plan.
No way out.
But I'm alive,
and that bastard didn't
get what he came for.
Yet.

Chapter 19
A Fire Lit

The coal baron Indrid Cold sent a dozen agents to evict a
miner's family from company housing. The sheriff and the mayor
disagreed. The massacre that followed left the mayor dead, two
miners slain, and seven of Indrid's agents bleeding out in the dirt.
The sheriff was tried for murder. On the day of the sheriff's acquittal,
he was shot dead on the courthouse steps. That's what it took to
light the fuse.

Ten thousand men marched on Storm Mountain, armed, angry,
and wearing red kerchiefs knotted at their necks. Indrid's workers
had long clamored for unionization. The murder of their hero lit a
fire that couldn't be put out. The newly installed sheriff, along with
three thousand lawmen, company agents, and strikebreakers, went to
meet them.

Upon the mountain broke waves of meat and bone. The sea of
red kerchiefs charged into rhythmic bursts of automatic gunfire.
Private planes circled overhead, dropping military ordnance through
the storm clouds. American bombs, falling on Americans. In
America. Land of the free.

The bombs screamed as they fell. Then, one bomb missed. It
tore through the clouds already crackling with static and the sky
erupted. A coal vein deep and long ignited with the fury of a

dragon's breath, like something old, and wrong, had woken up beneath them. A fire that never truly died.

In the end, it wasn't justice the miners found. Just the feds. Federal troops descended upon the red kerchiefs, forcing surrender at gunpoint. A hundred dead. A thousand charged with treason. The injured, innumerable. Years later, the men who stood tall against the coal baron are forgotten. Their moniker twisted into a mockery. A punchline. An embarrassment. The redneck.

They say Indrid Cold was there that day, watching from the ridge like a king at war. They say when his mine caught fire, he ran in screaming and desperate to save his precious power. They say no one ever saw him again, but I did.

When I was a child, my father used to tell me stories of the old times before the coal wars, before the battle that turned the mine into a sleeping, belching dragon. My father didn't have much, but he still had the mountain. After serving in the army he took what little he saved up back to the mountain with a dream. The company houses stood hollow on the hillsides, empty and unsteady, like they were forgetting what they used to be. Da wanted to fix it up, give it new life. Make it a ski village. We lived in a small trailer, the three of us, with the best view in the whole damn country, far as I'm concerned. We were happy. Until he stepped out of the mine.

He came from the dragon's mouth, black as a walking shadow. Smoke clung to him like skin.

And when he turned his face to me, I saw it.

That impossible grin. Bleached bone teeth behind a smile that didn't belong to a man. I froze. My father didn't.

He screamed for me to run. To hide. It was the first time I ever heard fear in his voice. Also the last. I buried myself in the tall grass.

Trembling. Small. From the hollow of that field, I watched him. The smiling shadow, kill my mother. My father fought, tried to stop him, died doing it. The mountain took pity on me that day, wrapped my screams in the wind and sent them tumbling down into the holler. Lost in the trees.

Chapter 20
Salamander Bride

I wake in a hard, cold void. Strong, clammy hands paw at my feet—gripping, pulling—dragging me away from the faint purpling light of dawn seemingly miles above my head. Does he have me? Am I caught? I hear voices in the distance. High-pitched and small. Like insects arguing across water, but the creature at my feet is silent.

I thrash, kicking wildly, slamming my head against the narrow stone that presses me in on all sides. My hands are pinned. I can't move. Can't reach my flashlight. Can't reach my gun. I'm stuck. Terror floods through me, crashing in fast and breathless. I start to hyperventilate. Breathe. Slow it down. I try. I try. But panic doesn't care. I awkwardly inch forward like some wounded thing— squirming through the rock, scraping, crawling. The hands return.

Cold fingers clamp around my swollen ankles, grip tight and yank. I'm pulled through with a violent lurch, then go limp, flopping like dead weight onto stone. I hit chin-first. Teeth clap shut with a crack. The floor is smooth. Hard. Cool as anything I've ever felt. I roll, breath ragged, and grope for the flashlight. Click. A weak yellow beam cuts through the dark. The cave is wider now. Much wider. In the black beyond my light, it feels eternal. I scan the chamber: Stalactites hang like teeth from the ceiling. Stalagmites jab up from the floor like stone spears. A small stream cuts through the middle, thin, fast, and whispering secrets to the stone. Above me, the ceiling stretches out like some ancient chandelier, too high to light, too old to move.

Then I feel her. The owner of the clammy hands.

She stands beside me, silent and unnoticed until I stumble backward onto the stone again. Her frame is long and thin, wrapped in skin so pale and translucent it's barely there. Her breasts hang small and flat against a cage of ribs. Her hair is long, dark, and limp like river weeds hanging in the shallows. Where her eyes should be, only skin. No sockets. No lids. Just smooth, stretched flesh, unbroken. She's a distorted funhouse reflection of a woman, but still a woman. I don't understand. I steady my breath, slow and deliberate, and rise to my feet. Every rustle, every shift of weight sounds like thunder in the silence.

She doesn't move, but I know she's listening. I don't know this tale or this creature. Maybe no one does. She doesn't seem like the others. She's from here, from beneath.

"Do you talk?" I ask her softly.

No response.

"You have kin?" I ask again, just above a whisper.

She raises one long, cold finger and presses it hard against my lips. Silence. She's telling me to hush. The tinny voices I heard before begin to echo through the cavern again, closer now, bouncing off the stone in strange, shrill patterns.

But I know the sound this time. I lean in and gently wrap my fingers around her wrist, guiding her hand down.

I whisper: "You kind of remind me of a salamander, so I'm gonna call you Miss Sally. That alright with you?"

She doesn't answer.

"I'm sorry for bein' so forward. I don't usually go 'round grabbin' on nekid ladies I just met in the dark, but..."

The voices are getting louder, sharper, now.

"...we gotta get out of here. We got goblins comin' our way. You know a way out?"

She doesn't answer only turns, slowly, her thin neck stretching, head cocked toward the black beyond the stalagmites. Then she moves, silent as mist, gliding barefoot across the cold stone, her long limbs flowing like water, pale skin catching the yellow of my flashlight just enough to look ghostlit. I follow. She weaves through the rock like she's been doing it a thousand years.

The voices grow behind us, goblin-chatter, high and sharp like teeth on glass. Tommyknockers. They're hunting. Sally presses a hand to the wall, a smooth section of stone I would've passed right by, and a narrow slit opens. Just wide enough for a man to slip through sideways. I wedge in, flashlight tucked beneath my chin, scraping against the stone with every breath. The passage bends and twists, the air wet and cold and full of old smells—moss, sulfur, rot. Sally moves ahead, barefoot and soundless. Eventually, the stone opens again. A small cavern with a ceiling like cathedral ribs and a pool of perfectly still black water. She stops at the edge. And finally... she turns to face me. There's something in the way she tilts her head, the way she lifts one hand toward the far wall. An invitation. A goodbye. There, nested between two massive slabs of quarts, two wood planks make a sloped passage. Faint daylight filters down through a broken vent, slanting in like a heaven-sent thread. It leads out. I turn to thank her. But she's already fading into the dark.

"No," I whisper. "Come on. Come with me."

She pauses and presses one long finger to her lips.

Hush. Behind us, the voices are too close now, rising in shrieks and hissing tones, echoing with knocking claws and wet, slapping feet.

Then she glides backward as I watch the black swallow her completely. She saved me, and I have to believe that she knows how to stay safe from those things. That she went back for a reason. I run. I claw my way up the passage. Up the stone ramp. Through a hatch that smells of iron and hay. I tumble out into the light. The kind that pierces your eyes like a javelin. A field. Frozen dew. Dead grass. Chickens scatter from the edge of a sagging farmstead. I collapse in the dirt, staring up at the rising sun.

Chapter 21
Man Eating Goblins

I walk slow, limping through the frost-laced field toward the farmhouse. Gun in hand, tucked in the pocket of my sweatshirt. Don't want to spook the owners. Don't want to be taken unawares, either. The place is old. Weather-worn. Paint flaking off in long tired strips. Windows dark. Could be abandoned. Could be sleeping. Could be worse.

The morning light glints off the barrel of a rusted wind vane spinning lazy on the roof. Somewhere inside, a radio faintly crackles to life, staticky gospel bleeding through the boards. I continue creeping along the exterior wall, slow and ready, with one boot dragging behind me like a busted wheel. My body aches like something chewed and spit out by the dark, but I'm still standing.

Through the window, I spot her. The young blond, Bex, fussing with some kind of radio console. Old mic rig. Antenna stretching from the roof like a branch desperate to touch the sky. She's alive. They're alive. Beside her, I hear the unmistakable gurgle of Squonk. I limp up to the window and tap it gently. She spins with a start, a chipped kitchen knife clutched tight in one hand.

But the moment she sees me, her posture collapses. The fight in her melts like frost in sunlight. Relief floods her face. Her eyes brighten. She smiles. I limp around to the front door. They must've barricaded it during the night. Chairs, a small table, maybe an old dresser, all piled up behind it. Out beyond the house, there's a single dirt trail—a narrow lane carving its way through frostbitten fields. No sign of civilization in any direction.

Squonk squeezes through the barricade with a wet squish, wrapping himself around my leg like a damp, loyal cankle. Inside, I hear the groaning scrape of wood on wood, furniture dragged aside with effort and haste. Then the door creaks open. Bex stands there. And before I can get a word out, she throws herself into me—arms tight, heart pounding against my chest, her warmth nearly toppling my unsteady frame. She pulls me inside. Slams the door shut behind us. I stagger forward and collapse into the first chair I find at the kitchen table. The room smells like dust, coffee grounds and old wood.

After sitting a spell, I finally ask, "How'd you end up here?"

"Fanny, she left us here."

I nod, thinking aloud. "She knows the lay of the land. Might be the only place she knew folks might be."

Bex hesitates. Her voice is low, uncertain.

"How'd you...? Is it over?"

I sigh, long and deep. "It is for you."

She doesn't argue.

"We'll wait it out," I add. "Then head back to your car. You drive me to town, a different town. We'll make our way from there... Any idea where the owners are?"

She moves to the counter, grabs a box of cereal, and pours it into a bowl with slow, careful hands. Runs some water from the tap over it, then hands me the bowl with a tarnished spoon.

"Don't know," she says. "The milk's expired."

I take it without question. Toss the spoon onto the table. Sink back into the chair. Tilt the bowl to my face and slurp the softening slurry down my gullet. It's plain. Wholesome. And the best damn thing I've had in what feels like days.

Squonk waddles up beside me, eyes soft, breath low. He gurgles once, then nestles against my leg. He's trying to tell me something, in the way only Squonk can.

"Told her to head for the mountain?" I ask quietly.

He squonks once. Affirmative. I pat his head with a tenderness I don't show most folks, not knowing if Fanny coming to the mountain is a blessing... or a curse. I finish the last of the cereal, then rise with a grunt and clatter the bowl into the sink.

"There's a radio?" I ask, already moving toward the console. "I need to get the ape on the horn."

"I've been trying all morning," Bex says, standing off to the side. "Don't know how it works. Can't reach anyone."

I sink into the worn seat. Slide on the yellowed plastic headphones. The cushions crackle like old skin against my ears. The radio hums a low, patient growl. I twist the tuner slowly to the left. The simian supremacist'll want his signal out front. But there's nothing. Just static. I squeeze the trigger on the mic. An empty sort of silence fills my ears.

"Yaya. Come in, Yaya."

I release.

Static bubbles back in and I squeeze again.

"Come in, Yaya."

"Ahoy ahoy! Yellowtop here."

The big voice cuts through the white noise, warm and ridiculous and familiar. Before I can breathe, the moment is shattered. A guttural, raw, feral scream rips through the field outside, piercing the walls of the farmhouse like a blade. I squeeze the mic harder.

"Trouble. Flatwoods. Farmstead. Big antenna. Come quick... Indrid's back."

Bex is hollering for me from the front window. Squonk is right beside her, squealing with alarm. The last words I heard before ripping off the headphones are, "Wait, I–" But I don't. Furniture legs scrape across a groaning wood floor, as I heave the couch away from the front door.

I sprint out the door into the autumn morning's sun on busted shins and ballooning ankles. Every step is a knife. Every stomp is fire through bone, but I run across the frozen ground toward her, Miss Sally. Those goblin cunts caught her. They're dragging her into the sunlight. Her naked gossamer-pale skin blisters under the open sky. Smoke rises from her shoulders like burnt paper. She can't be here. She writhes and screams, as a dozen metallic turquoise goblins drag her against the dead grass. Tommyknockers. Ugly little bastards with needle claws, swinging crude stone hammers and hooting like devils.

I reach her, and my right boot collides into the closest tommy with every ounce of hatred I've got. It flies into a trunk of a nearby tree and drops limp. Another's yanking her by the hair. I stomp its spine with both feet. Feel the crack, but one of them's on me now. Its needle claws stab into my calf, deep and burning. I scream and fall ripping the thing out of my leg and toss it across the grass. My hands are shaking. My blood's hot and running.

Miss Sally's still fighting, flailing wildly, skin boiling in the autumn sun. She can't see what she's fighting, but doesn't stop. And I'm face-down in the grass, staring up at another tommy. It's standing over me. Hammer raised high.

"They look bigger from down here", I think.

As the creature swings down toward my unguarded face, I slap it away with everything I've got. It tumbles, crashing to the ground in a heap of limbs and shrieking metal. I don't give it time, I army crawl toward it, dragging my shredded leg through the dirt. It's dazed, but moving, trying to rise. I lunge on top of it. Raise my fist and bring it down. Again. And again. And again.

Each strike crunches deeper. Its shining metallic skin doesn't break, but what's underneath turns to mush. A lumpy, twitching sack of ruin. I shove myself up off the ground, chest heaving.

Miss Sally, beside me, smashes one tommy's skull down against a stone until it stops moving. I take turquoise stained hands and pull her thin elongated frame up on to her bare feet. The only flesh spared from burns rests below her long black locks of hair cascading down from her eyeless head.

There's maybe six or seven left now. They move too quick to count. They flit between trees and shadows like angry wasps. Then, Bex. She charges in beside us, breath ragged and eyes blazing. In her hands, a rusted iron claw rake and a garden hoe. Smart girl.

She jams the rake under me, bracing my weight. Then swings the hoe like the Grim Reaper's scythe across a battlefield. With this reprieve, I strip off my jacket and shirt and grab Sally's blistered, trembling hand.

"Miss Sally, it's me. I got ya."

I pull the layers down over her, raising the hood of my sweater, wrapping her as best I can with my red and blue blood stained cotton garments. Only her lower legs remain bare. But it's enough to buy time. To keep her from the worst of it. I glance at her, offer half a grin. "Hope your sense of smell ain't as good as your hearing."

I grip the rake like a crutch, leaning heavy on the twisted metal, and start guiding Sally toward the house. Her legs wobble with uncertainty under her. She stumbles with every step, but she moves.

More of the damned goblins pour out of the cavern now, spilling into the daylight like a swarm of angry hornets. Bex lets out a sharp squeal and stumbles back, recoiling from the onslaught.

I shout, "Squonk!"

And like an overripe cannonball, he explodes from the doorway, sprinting across the field like a fat show dog at full tilt. He skids through the dirt, circles around Sally once, and begins nudging her forward—chirping, gurgling, and guiding. She listens. She follows. Together, they move toward the house, slow but steady.

I grip the rake a little tighter and turn to face the tide. Bex swings the hoe wild, teeth bared, hair matted with sweat. Tommy's cling to the shaft—clawing, gnawing, screeching. She's overwhelmed. I plant a foot, raise the rake high above my head and bring it down hard. The tines tear through a cluster, impaling two and crushing another beneath the blow. I wrench it free and swing again. And again. Wild, desperate, brutal. We're not winning. They're too many. Too fast. Ol' Snarly would've loved this. Plenty of squeaking chew toys to rip apart.

Bex screams as she rips a tommy off her back and hurls it to the ground. It scrambles to rise and I stomp the flat of the rake across its forehead with a sickening crack. It stops moving. But more are coming, so many more.

"Get back to the house! Now!" I shout.

She looks at me with hesitation in her eyes. I swing the rake in a wide arc, steel catching bone and dirt as they circle tighter.

"I'm right behind you. Go!" I bellow again.

She runs while I skewer three more. In the distance I hear the front door slam and a wave of relief catches me for a moment, before—

Crack. Something slams the back of my skull. Sharp. Precise. A perfect little tommy-knock. The ground rushes up to meet me. My face hits turquoise-stained dirt.

Everything goes black. And in the dark... I'm falling. An endless red sky unfolds above me. An impossibly vast sea below. The sea of souls, my final resting place. Beside me, a cliffside taller than anything is just outside my reach. I fell for what seems like forever, but I'm never any closer to the waves. The world falls with me, to where, I do not know.

I reach for the cliff and come to on my back. Thin nylon ropes dig into my arms and chest, pinning me flat to the dirt. A tommy sits perched on my sternum, tranquil and watching me with unblinking eyes. He's a fancy one, wearing a gold Rolex across his body like a sash. Must be a leader of some sort. Its skin shines that sick turquoise under the high sun.

I take a breath. "Y'all don't seem to have a bug in your bonnet," I say, trying on a smirk. "So, why you hasslin' us?"

The creature tilts its head, then answers in a tinny little voice like a busted toy speaker.

"He don't give those out willy-nilly. Too slow to lay, too slow to hatch... for the likes of us, anyway."

It sniggers, tapping one claw idly against my chest.

"But long as we work for him? Things stay smooth."

I glance to the side at the field littered with twitching turquoise corpses.

"This is smooth?"

"Better than the alternative."

My smile fades.

"Why does he want the Thunderbird?"

My voice is flat. No humor left. The tommy shrugs an exaggerated little puppet motion.

"No idea. Somethin' about how we all got here. Says he can get us home." It leans down, close enough I can smell its breath, wet metal and bile. "Now that we got you... he might even keep that promise."

"You're forgetting one thing," I say, calm as a cloud, resting my head back in the grass.

The tommy blinks, its little head cocking sideways.

"Oh? And what's that?"

I don't answer. Just breathe. I Settle deeper into the binds, like I'm laying down to nap. The creature shifts on my chest.

"What am I forgetting?" it screeches, its tinny little voice shrill with sudden panic.

I laugh. It snarls and jabs a needle claw into the scar on my cheek.

"Tell me."

I wince but hold steady.

Then I whisper, slow and cool, "Come closer."

The gremlin leans in, smug and curious.

"My name ain't Gulliver." My neck snaps forward, jaw wide, and I clamp down on its ugly little head with everything I've got. Teeth grind against bone. A wet crunch. Then pop. My mouth fills with something bitter and thick, turquoise ink, warm and pulsing. I spit. Then smile, bloody and wild. I grunt and twist, pushing and pulling against the nylon bindings. They weren't meant to hold someone like me. Not for long. I pocket the gold watch. "Gold for wolves," I tell myself.

Across the field, the goblins, what's left of them, are busy. They're stacking their dead in neat little piles. Methodical. Mechanical. There are fewer of them now. Some must've run, scuttled back down the hole to report their victory. Idiots. The closest tommy finally notices the commotion. It opens its mouth to scream, but doesn't get the chance. My hand comes down, mottled green and purple, swollen and broken, and lands hard on its back, driving it into the dirt. My fingers tighten. I feel its bones bend and then pop. Its skull disconnects from its spine like a cork pulled from a bottle.

I let the body drop. No one stacks me. The next one's a daydreamer. Whistling to himself like a dwarf in some twisted Disney cartoon. He's facing away, lost in the rhythm of his work. Stacking corpse after corpse with perfect, patient care. I move slow. Army-crawling through the dirt, ribs grinding, breath low. Turquoise blood froths on my lips—bitter, warm, and still bubbling from the last one. It drips in fat drops from my chin. The little bastard hums a tune that doesn't belong in this world. Light and bouncy, like he's building a house out of bones and smiles. And I crawl closer. Closer.

He notices me when my shadow falls across his work. He turns slowly with shock in his eyes, the whistle dying on his lips. I rise to my knees in front of him, towering like some great behemoth. The blood of his kin froths and drips from my mouth, stringing down my chin in globs of green. He's frozen. Too afraid to run. I reach down and lift him with one hand. He kicks once, feebly. In that tinny little voice, I hear a single, desperate word: "Please..." I grip his lower half with one hand, his upper with the other. And I pull. Pop. Like a party cracker made of bone and bile.

The few creatures that remain skitter across the field like roaches in the light away from the house, away from me, all but one. He doesn't run, he screams a ragged, high-pitched cry, guttural with sorrow, stumbling toward the mangled body at my feet, wailing a name I'll never understand. Drops to his tiny knees. Cradles what's left of his kin in his tiny arms. Rocking. Shaking. Weeping. It reminds me of that day. I watch him. Silent. I raise my boot and bring it down. The sound is wet and final.

I turn and limp toward the house.

Chapter 22
Spitting Venom

I sit on the front porch steps and breathe the venom out of my lungs. Slowly, the world returns. My field of vision widens. Color seeps back in, like paint bleeding into water.

Bex steps out with the first aid kit clutched in both hands. She tells me she got the 'eyeless woman' settled in a dark room, blackout curtains pulled tight. She used what little burn ointment we had. Says Squonk's curled up beside her, watching over her. I suspect Squonk'll do her more good than any tube of ointment. Bex sits next to me, but her voice feels a thousand miles away. How did he know my name? The thought circles like a buzzard.

Pain snaps me back. Bex has a pair of small pliers gripping one of those long, needle-like claws embedded in my back. She gives it a yank, and the world flashes white.

I grunt and take the pliers from her. My turn. I work on the barbs still lodged in my thigh, jaw tight. She rummages through the kit again, pulls out alcohol and bandages. We patch each other up in silence.

The sting of the rubbing liquor hits like fire. She tapes gauze over my gouges. I finish with the leg, splash alcohol straight onto the wounds, and grit through it.

Then I take her hand and guide her down onto the lower step between my knees, her back to me. Red and turquoise smears streak down her back and arms soaking into her ruined shirt. I gather her long blonde hair, matted with sweat and gore, and sweep it gently over her shoulder.

I work the claw from her neck. Her ribs. The back of her arms. She flinches now and then, but doesn't say a word.

I dab each wound with antiseptic, the cotton turning the color of rust. One cut runs deep and jagged. I reach for the super glue, draw a thin bead down the split skin, and pinch the flesh together with careful fingers. It reminds me of Yaya patching my face together when I was still just a boy. That damn ape is still hours away.

My undershirt's little more than rags stained with sickly patterns that might be mistaken for a tie dye. I gather the remaining cloth in a bunch and with a long pull, the fabric tears away like paper.

"Thank you." I tell Bex without looking at her.

"Don't mention it."

In the field, the pile of corpses lie still. Their strange, metallic skin catches the afternoon light. Silver and glistening, barely scratched despite the carnage. I rise, sore and slow, and head for the barn for tools.

Hours pass. One by one, I skin the tommyknockers, peeling them like trout, careful to keep the hides intact. Flesh comes away easy enough. It's the sewing that grinds me down. Beside my makeshift fire pit, I thread slick twine through a needle, made from a claw torn from my side, and begin stitching the skins into a limp cylinder. Tedious work, the kind that lets your mind run while your hands are busy. The kind I hate.

Bex sits nearby, quiet beside the fire. She's bundled in an old woman's faded floral wool coat, too big for her, sleeves rolled up. The light from the flames flickers across her cheeks as she watches me.

I finish the stitch and hold the patchwork tube up to the firelight. It glints wet and eerie. I hang it on a hook above the pit, letting the smoke rise into it, funneling through the seams. The dusky sky fills with that thick, earthy haze—burnt wood, blood, and grease.

I sit beside her on a broken stool. The fire pops.

"He should've been here by now," I say, finally breaking the silence.

"He'll come," she replies, her hand resting soft and warm on my arm. I watch the smoke swirl.

"There's no telling when, or if, they'll come back," I say after a while. "I don't want to be asleep when they do."

Night falls. The tube of skin stiffens in the smoke, drying into a crusted sheath. When I touch it, it crackles, rigid, but with some flex. Usable at least.

Miss Sally sits outside on the porch, away from the firelight but not far off. Just close enough to listen. Maybe she wants to feel less alone in this unwalled world she was dragged into. I couldn't tell you. She rocks gently in one of the old wooden chairs, my sweatshirt crumpled underneath her translucent, naked form. Squonk gurgles and coos in her lap, little hands clinging to her as if he knows she needs the weight.

The boards creak beneath us as Bex and I step onto the porch, the leather tube of stitched tommy skin clutched in my hand like a relic. We settle into the remaining rockers beside her, the three of us in a line, watching the wind move through the tall grass.

No one speaks. The porch light hums faintly. The fire crackles behind the screen door and somewhere in the night, a mourning dove sings too late for the hour. Not a word passes between us. But the silence is thick with meaning. With questions unspoken. With strange kinship.

Sally shifts, and places her hand on my arm. I finally break the silence and with a cough, I start to introduce our troop of misfits.

"Miss Sally, that's Bex there to your left. She's the one who patched you up. I see you've made fast friends with Squonk, here."

He's curled up in her lap, gurgling contentedly, his watery eyes half-lidded with peace. Sally rests a thin, translucent hand on his back, her rocking steady, like she's been doing it all her life.

"I'm Carl, you saved me in that cave of yours... I'm not sure when it'll be safe for you to return there."

I take the stitched tube of metallic leather and begin cutting the threads, unfolding it into a flat sheet of turquoise, shimmering dully in the firelight.

"I reckon I got enough material here for you," I murmur.

I thread a new line through two rough holes at the edge of the unwieldy quilt of skin, my fingers working the claw-needle slow and steady.

"Cryptid hunter AND seamstress?" Bex says, her voice dry. She gives me an incredulous look.

"Been patchin' clothes and tannin' hides since I was a youngin', " I tell her.

Headlights slice through the dark, bright and sudden. They cut long, warped shadows across the barn and up the trees. A tall trail of dust churns behind the approaching vehicle, curling like smoke in the night air.

I don't stop rocking. The patchwork quilt rests in my lap. My hand finds the blued steel of the revolver tucked in the waistband of my pants. My thumb strokes the hammer. Only three bullets, I remind myself. Quiet. Patient. Waiting.

A truck door creaks open, then slams twice with a shudder that rocks the frame. The headlights still glare, blinding and full of dust. For a moment, the figure behind them is nothing more than a silhouette.

The truck groans as it shifts under his weight.

"Y'know," a familiar, booming voice calls through the dark, "I had a hell of a time findin' this place."

Yaya. I take my hand off the hammer and let the breath out slow. Relief spreads warm through my chest, and I smile without meaning to.

"Took ya long enough," I shout back.

Before I can say more, Bex is already running toward him, arms wide. She throws herself into a hug around the massive ape-man, nearly bouncing off his chest.

Miss Sally doesn't move. She listens, head tilted ever so slightly, eyes focused on the sound, her expression soft and distant like she's hearing the voice of an old friend in a dream.

"Miss Sally... I see you ain't got any shame bout bein' buck nekid." I keep my voice low and gentle. "Don't bother me none, but I made you somethin' on account of your kindness this mornin.'" She turns slightly toward me and I see her tears and blisters are already healing in the night's sky. "Those lil' vermin treated ya mighty unkind, but now they can make it up to you." I take her hands, light as air, and help her to her feet. Her skin is cool, almost not there. I drape the patchwork of metallic pelts around her narrow shoulders, shimmering like oil in firelight. The toggle slips through its loop, snug, and I tug the hood over her head. It hides most of her face, except for the small smile curling at the corners of her mouth.

"There ya go," I whisper returning the smile. "Anytime ya find yourself out in the sun, ya remember to take yer cover-all."

I squeeze her shoulders gently, then stoop to grab my shredded sweatshirt and the rucksack off the porch. Squonk is already padding beside us, stubby feet squelching softly on the wood.

As we step off the porch, Yaya calls from the truck, voice loud and teasing, "put a shirt on, ya creep!"

Then his tone shifts, curiosity piqued. "And who's this shimmering creature?"

The patchwork cloak bounces the headlights' beams like disco lights on a bar's last call, flashing across the porch and the gravel, making the shadows dance.

"She don't talk much," I say. "call her Miss Sally. You don't know her?"

He squints, tilting his head.

"She ain't one of ours," he says with a shrug.

"What do you mean?" Bex interjects.

"We gotta get outta here before more trouble comes," I say, tightening the strap on my rucksack. "Bex, you ride shotgun. Sally takes the middle seat with Squonk, they seem to get along. Yellowtop, you're driving. I'll ride in the bed."

Yaya grins, already sliding behind the wheel. "Good, I left a surprise back there for ya."

I drop the tailgate and there it is. My duffel, stuffed fat with my dad's old military service rifle and boxes of ammunition. I run a hand over the familiar canvas, lips twitching into a smile.

"Good monkey," I mutter under my breath.

Then, hot breath on my face. A massive, rasping tongue drags up my cheek, leaving a trail of slobber and the scent of wet ash and brimstone.

I freeze and then grin.

"Ol' Snarly," I say, chuckling low in my throat.
"You missed a hell of a time."

The clouds slip past the moon, and pale light spills across the yard. Her big yellow eyes gleam back at me, wide as fists. An impossibly large black dog, more shadow than flesh. The fur on her shoulders stirs like wind through tall grass. I nuzzle her massive head, scratch behind one ear. She groans, heavy and content, and drops down into the bed with a loud thump.

I climb in beside her, pull the gate shut, and settle in for the long ride. My head rising and falling with the slow rhythm of her breath.

"Where we headed?" Yaya hollers from the cab,
engine already rumbling.

PART 3:
THE ONE-EYED SERPENT

Chapter 23
Time Heals Some

It's mid-December and cold. Snow's deep up here on the mountain, and it hasn't let up in days. I keep the fire going steady all the same. It's been about a month since the farmhouse, and I'm mostly healed up. Good enough to get by at least. Still stiff in the mornings. Sore in strange places. My skin's got green patches here and there, bruised or blood-poisoned, who knows. Doubt any of it made me any prettier.

We got Bex her car back. It wasn't too bad off. The hollowmen only slashed one tire. Just enough to keep us from making a getaway if we'd reached it. I changed it for her while she stood watch, then she was on her way back to her life. She had to get back to her classes. She came down to write a paper, after all. She didn't say much about what happened in Flatwoods. I think she was a bit shaken. Getting held hostage by some undead smiling freak, then getting rescued by an angelic cuttlefish only to have to square up against a bunch of yard gnomes can do that to a person. She just left, quiet like. I didn't let it bother me.

We took Miss Sally up the mountain since her cavern was overrun. She didn't seem to mind. Didn't take her long to find a crack in the mountain's stone walls and slither right inside. For someone who never speaks, the world feels quieter without her around. I catch Squonk whimpering and pawing at her crevice now and again, hopeful. Like he misses her more than the rest of us.

There've been sightings of Fanny's lights at night in the woods. But really these days, it's just me, the boys, and Snarly of course. Probably for the best. Snarly's the only girl I need. She don't talk much. Doesn't ask a bunch of questions, doesn't confuse and complicate things. Yaya and I, we're no closer to figuring out where the Thunderbird is or guessing Indrid's next move. No closer to any of it. The tommyknocker said it was a way home. I'm sure that's what the tommys want, but doubt that son of a bitch has any intention of delivering on it.

It's nearing midday, and I'm planted in my aluminum folding chair, bundled up in my patched sweatshirt, watching the thin thread of black smoke curl and twirl from the dragon's mouth of the mine. I know something terrible is going to happen. I just don't know what. Or when. Or how to stop it. My eyes get heavy, and the blue sky starts to fill with pink.

Squealing tires snap me out of the trance. I stand up slow and wander toward the ledge, peering down the mountain. Below, a cheap little green Ford is stuck halfway up the slope, spinning its tires uselessly in the snow.

"Yaya!" I holler back over my shoulder. "Get your ass in gear. A lady needs a tow!"

I whistle, sharp and clear. The snow breaks like thunder. Tremors roll underfoot as huge prints appear in the powder, one after the next, tearing toward me. I run my hand through Snarly's coat, grab tight onto her thick mane and straddle the air. Lifted into the sky and and tearing down the mountain on a violent wake of wind and powder.

The green Ford's still spinning in place, but the frustrated scowl inside has shifted, first to shock at my apparent levitation, then to a wide smile of something dangerously close to delight. Bex. I hop off Snarly, brushing the snow from my sleeves, a little embarrassed by the whole display. Caught myself too excited and showing off for the girl.

Bex rolls down the window, grinning.

"A little help?" she says.

I nod and give a small hand signal, then slide into the passenger seat beside her. A moment later, the snowbank her car is buried in explodes, torn upward in great clumps and flung into the air. The whole car rocks violently as Snarly digs in, invisible and unstoppable. Snow splashes across the windshield like we're in another blizzard.

"Yaya'll be down in a bit with the tow," I say, still catching my breath. I glance at her, trying to sound casual.

"So... what's new? How've you been?" I ask too fast, too eager. I clear my throat, reel it back in. "Didn't think we'd be seein' you again."

"I've been good," she says with a smirk. "And you're not getting rid of me that easily." She leans in, just enough for her voice to go soft. "I've got news. Something that might help."

After Yaya tows us up to camp, we settle in around the fire. I pour a little bitter black for the three of us. Squonk, stiff from the cold but buzzing with joy at his friend's return, trundles through the snow and curls up at Bex's feet, warming his blobby frame by the fire.

"It's so very nice to have a pretty face back in camp for once," Yaya says with a sly grin, cupping his mug in both hands. "How'd your paper do?"

Bex scoffs. "Well, my journalism professor tore my paper to shreds, but it did pretty well in my creative writing class." She takes a sip of the coffee, wincing a little at the strength. "Anyway, I kept researching after I got back. I think I found something useful. Might help you."

"Oh, that's wonderful, my dear," Yaya says dramatically. "This boy's been lovesick and useless these last few weeks."

"Shut it," I growl, glaring into my cup.

Bex raises an eyebrow at me, but doesn't push. She turns her attention to Yaya instead.

"Before I get into what I found," she says, voice tightening as she straightens up, "I've got some questions for you. Will you allow me to interview you?"

"O' course, my dear. Since you're holding your information as leverage, we are at your mercy." Yaya quips.

She starts right into it. "Awhile back, you mentioned Miss Sally wasn't one of 'yours'. What did you mean by that?"

Yaya takes a long breath and leans back in his chair. He stares into the fire for a while before speaking.

"Squonk, myself, Fanny, the moth character—"

"Mortimer." I interrupt.

"Others too," he says, gesturing vaguely out toward the valley. "We're all orphans, of a kind. Refugees, if you like. From the same place."

"You're alien?" She asks.

"We're from here."

He pauses.

"But not here here. You understand?"

"Those trolls wanted to go ho—" Bex starts.

"Tommyknockers," I correct her.

"Pukwudgie," Yaya corrects me, without missing a beat.

"They wanted to go home," she finishes.

"Yes," I say, flat.

"Your home?" she asks, looking at Yaya.

He nods once. "Yes."

"And Miss Sally... isn't from there?"

"As far as I know, no. I can't say I know every creature from my world. But I know a fair few. Sally... doesn't match anything I recognize."

There's a silence, broken only by the crackle of wood. Bex shifts forward a little.

"What's the deal with the bugs?"

Yaya sighs again, slower this time.

"Skudagaya. Burrow-spirits. Rot demons. Here they're called carrion bugs, or devil bugs if you like. They tend to go after the small animals. Typically the dead and the dying. Puppet the bodies like marionettes." He trails off, visibly more tired now. Eyes gone distant.

"They've got some kind of hive-mind thing going," I add, voice low. "He, Indrid, was tryin' to infest me for info."

Bex's eyes widen, just a little.

"I don't know if it works both ways," I say. "Not interested in finding out."

She pauses for a moment, watching Yaya carefully, then asks her final question, the one that's clearly been burning a hole in her ever since she came back up this mountain. "What does the Thunderbird have to do with getting home?"

The words hang there in the cold air between us, untouched by the fire's warmth.

Chapter 24
Cracking Skies

The sky is raw and seething, the color of open wounds. A storm-split sky. Below, the forests are filled, not with walnut and hickory, but with impossibly old pawpaw and strange broad-leafed trees that I've never seen. Out of the strange forest, they climb. Hundreds of creatures, each one strange. Each one wrong in its own way. Too many legs. Too few eyes. Feathers where there ought to be fur. Horns, scales, soft shells, slime. Oddities that would never congregate, side by side trudging up Storm Mountain. My mountain.

Behind them comes the swarm of hollows. Friends, families, their kin, now hosts. All mouths pulled back into a frozen, rictus smile as they ascend toward the living like a tide of rot. The air is thick with fear. The ground with desperation. The survivors come to the mountain for refuge, for one last chance. And above, unmoving, the Thunderbird waits. It sits alone on the summit, vast and still, cloaked in swirling clouds shot through with lightning. Its eyes like burning suns, peering down from its perch.

Squonk, Fanny, Snarly Yow, hundreds more. Strangers shrinking from their inevitable fate. Yaya climbs with them toward a storm, hoping for the mercy of a benevolent god. The refugees push through exhaustion, dragging themselves up the jagged spine of the mountain. A great feathered serpent wheels through the blood-red sky, its massive wings beating thunder into the air. With talons wide as tree trunks, it swoops down again and again, collecting stragglers too slow to climb and lifting them gently to a familiar plateau near where a mine should be.

Thunderheads bloom across the heavens, black and boiling, swallowing what's left of the sky. Lightning lashes down in jagged bursts, white against the crimson haze. Each crack splits the world open. Each roll of thunder shakes the mountain beneath their feet like the bones of a waking god.

Yaya, the great blond beast, grits his teeth and pushes on. He's shoulder-deep in snow and mud, straining against the weight of an enormous two-headed turtle. The turtle grunts and groans. Behind them, the horde closes in. Slow. Methodical. Tireless. They wear the faces of Yaya's brothers, his sisters, his old clan, dead but not resting. Their mouths stretch too wide, too sharp, grins pulled taut like skin about to split. They crawl like cockroaches over the turtle's shell, over Yaya's back.

Hands claw at him. Fists slam down. They drag him to the ground. Then, talons. Enormous, curved, and holy. The feathered serpent crashes through the swarm with a shriek, its talons tearing the crowd apart like paper. Its tail lashes like a whip, sweeping dozens of the grinning husks off the cliffside in a single violent arc. It scoops up the turtle and Yaya both, rising into the storm-churned sky. But some of the horde cling to its feathers—biting, stabbing, squirming. The beast writhes midair, flailing and screeching, spiraling into a death spin like a crocodile dragging prey beneath the water. Its grip tightens too much on Yaya. Ribs creak. Vision narrows. Then loosens—too loose—and the turtle slips free, plummeting like a stone. The sky spins. Yaya's limbs go numb. The last thing he sees is lightning curling through the clouds as the world fades to black. Yaya wakes, battered and sprawled on the summit.

The wind screams. The sky splits. Below him, the great winged serpent thrashes and writhes in the snow—its body a blur of feathers, scales, and blood. It wrestles with the swarm still clinging to its hide, snapping them up with a hooked beak, its tendrils whipping and pulling attackers into its maw. Yaya groans, pushes up on shaking limbs. His body screams protest, but he doesn't stop. Another grinning husk clings to the serpent's side, driving a shard of bone between its ribs. With a roar, Yaya lunges forward, grips the attacker with both hands, and rips it away. Flesh tears. Bones snap. The husk goes limp in his grasp. He tosses it into the wind.

Then he sees it. Overhead. Perched on the jagged spine of the summit, still and dark as stone, is a bird. An eagle, but impossibly large. Its wings are folded like thunderclouds. Its body as tall as a tower. It does not move. It does not speak. It simply watches. Lightning cracks the sky behind it, casting its silhouette in stark black against the bleeding red storm. And still it waits.

Another attacker has Yaya pinned. Fangs bared, grin wide. The killing blow raised. Then, pressure breaks. As if the weight of the world vanishes for a breathless instant. The attacker is pulled upward, lifted several feet into the air. Then wings comes down. Slow. Smooth. Like the arm of a god brushing ants from the earth.

A tsunami of wind flattens everything in its path. Yaya gasps, shielded by the mountain itself. Above, the Thunderbird circles its mountain, wings stretched black across the storm. Lightning falls in branching arcs, slamming into the earth and burning legions of the hollow ones. Entire lines of the grinning dead incinerate in an instant.

Yaya watches, frozen in astonishment. The god of these lands has awakened. And then, beneath the thunder, angry screaming voices surround him. The sky erupts again, this time not with lightning, but with the deafening percussion of small, repeated explosions. Gunfire. Something else is in the sky, roaring. Not bird. Not beast. The feathered serpent reappears, spiraling through the smoke. It dives, sweeping survivors into its talons. Carrying the broken and the damned. Yaya tries to stand.

The Thunderbird passes overhead again, its shadow engulfing the mountain like nightfall. Then, a lightning strike. Cracks. Explodes above the outstretched wings. It hits the Thunderbird square. White light swallows the world. Then black.

He doesn't know how long he's out. He only knows deep and spreading pain, like he was the one who caught the blast. Like it was him who shattered. Flat on his back and breathing through tender ribs, he opens his eyes. Above him, a blue sky. The storm is gone. The air is clean. The forest, unfamiliar to him, is walnut and hickory. He turns his head. On a low branch of a young paw paw tree, sits a vivid red bird, singing like nothing's happened at all.

Chapter 25
An Unmovable Feast

"I'm out of school for Christmas break," Bex says, poking at the fire with a stick. "I'm heading home to see my folks, but there's something happening out that way." I glance over from my chair, and she's already reaching into her coat. "I was about to hit the road when I read something that made me think it might be something up your alley."

She pulls out a thick sheet of paper, newspaper clippings pasted neatly across the surface. She hands it to me. I lean back and read. Headlines. Missing children. All the same town. Accounts of grief, confusion, small-town panic. Local police issuing the usual useless statements.

"Tragic, but—" I start, about to hand it back.

"Just keep reading," she says, firmer now.

So I do, and about halfway down the page, buried in a paragraph about a girl who came back, there it is. Not tale of indecency. Not stranger danger. Just a single word from the child's lips, whispered: Snallygaster.

I sit up straight, "Well, I'll be."

I pass the sheet over to Yaya, tapping the line with my finger. "Read this."

Yaya perks up at the sight of the name, but his eyes don't stay there. He scans upward, expression tightening.

"This doesn't make sense," he mutters under his breath.

"We still gotta check it out," I tell him.

"Yeah... yeah, we do," he says, quieter than usual.

"Thank you for bringing this to us," I say, turning to Bex.

She nods. "When I saw it, I knew I had to take the detour south and show you."

"You did good."

Yaya leans forward now, voice low and urgent. "Carl, we have to move on this. If anyone knows the bird's whereabouts... it's him. And if it's in the paper, your gran-pappy ain't far behind."

I exhale, slow. The weight settling into my ribs.

"We don't usually venture that far... east," I mutter.

"Come stay with my folks," Bex says hopeful. "They've got space. I'll smooth it over."

In what passes for a bathroom in my decrepit little trailer, I clean myself up the best I can. Throw on some clothes that don't smell like mildew and gunpowder. You could say it's my Sunday best, though I really don't know what day it is. I want to make a good impression on her folks, at least.

Yaya takes a dip in the stream, his massive shape wading in like a shaggy boulder. Bex kneels beside him, brushing out the knots and mats in his yellow fur, patient as a groomer giggling about who knows what. I load my rifle bag into the back of the truck. With one sharp whistle, a steaming mound of snow bursts open and the truck lurches and sags on its springs. I toss the tattered blue tarp over Snarly's hulking shape and cinch it down snug. The tailgate closes with a satisfying thunk.

Squonk wiggles around in my rucksack, getting settled and squonks at me to not forget to say goodbye. I walk to the stone wall that leads to the mountain summit and the circle of crackling clouds beyond it. I run my finger tips along the stone face until they find the narrow slit, she vanished into not long ago. I slide down into the crevice and walk down a crooked, narrow corridor into the black. After walking blind for several minutes, I stop myself. I wanted to flick on my flashlight and go hunt her down. See where she's hiding out. Discover her secrets. But I don't. instead my voice echos out into the void, "We'll be back in a few days." Squonk lets out a gentle squonk, his voice echoing softer, before I continue, "Yer in charge till we get back," I say with a smile. And then we go.

It's evening by the time we arrive. Streetlights flicker to life across the neighborhood, casting everything in a sickly amber glow. The stars shrink from places like this, where it's never truly dark. It seems worlds away from any Appalachian holler. Bex is beaming at the sight of her family home, even after all the warnings she gave on the ride out. Standing in the driveway, I feel shabby in the land of yuppies. I shift my weight and feel the dirt on my boots and the stink of the road still clinging to me. I shouldn't care. Usually, folks like this don't rattle me. Half the time I'm working some angle. But this feels different. Maybe it's because I'm not trying to run a game. Maybe it's just Bex. That thought alone makes me want to leave.

The house looks tidy from the outside. A manicured lawn sits stiff and square in front of it like a patch of plastic turf. The siding is pale and spotless. Big windows. Straight lines. It stands tall on a cramped little lot. Neighbors press in from both sides like they're jockeying for space. Everything about it feels cramped and calculated. Well, some folks don't grow up with forests, cliffs and stars. Some get fences, porch lights and trimmed hedges. Bex grew up boxed in, while I grew wild like a weed.

She fits her key into the door and opens it gently.

"Mom, Dad, I'm home!" she calls out, cheerful.

"I brought some... friends with me."

Her mother appears in a blink, rushing in with arms open and a bright, painted smile that falters only slightly when she clocks me. Then Yaya steps into the light behind me, wearing a flannel shirt stretched to its limit, a wool coat draped over his overalls, and a cap barely shading his face. He can almost pass for some two-bit circus freak trying to look respectable. Her mother's smile twitches.

"We expected you hours ago! And you brought a boy?" she says, eyes still wide. "Who are these fine gentlemen?"

Bex, bless her, somehow never got around to putting a story together. You can see the gears turning behind her eyes as she tries to land one on the fly.

"This is my friend from school," she says too quickly like she can erase the pause.

"Carl," I offer, stepping forward with a small nod. "Very nice to meet you, ma'am. What should I call you?"

She takes my hand, soft and a little cool, caught slightly off guard by the kindness in my eyes.

"Very nice to meet you, Carl. Please, call me Deborah."

The smile flickers genuine for a moment. Then her gaze slides up to the behemoth looming just behind me. Yaya stands in full get-up, his breath steady and silent. He must be hot as hell in all that. He'd be sweating up a storm, if he could.

"Deborah, this here's my cousin," I say easily. "Blondie."

Deborah raises an eyebrow.

"He's a gentle soul," I add, dropping my voice just enough. "Bit touched, if I do say. It's best not to stare. He's a bit sensitive about his... condition." I smile like this ain't the first time I've run this script. "We're headed a bit further down the way," I continue. "Bex said you wouldn't mind putting us up for the night."

Deborah glances at Bex for half a second. It's quick, but loaded. Bex meets her gaze with a big awkward smile. There's something unspoken passed between them, but neither says a word. Deborah turns back to me.

"Of course," she says, voice warm but carefully measured. "Please, make yourselves at home. Daddy's just finishing up dinner. I'll set some extra plates."

"Much appreciated, ma'am," I reply, polite as can be.

At the dinner table, the wooden chairs squeak and groan beneath Yaya's weight, protesting like they're seconds from giving up entirely. Squonk is curled up, hidden in my bag beside my feet, occasionally shifting with a soft wet sigh. Mr. Beaumont carves into the roast beef with grim efficiency, his face set like concrete.

"If someone had called ahead," he says, not looking up from the cutting board, "we could have prepared for visitors."

His tone aims squarely at Bex.

"It was a spur-of-the-moment thing," I cut in, trying to take the edge off. "We don't want to put anyone out."

Mr. Beaumont's mouth pulls tight. He exhales through his nose and pastes on a strained smile.

"It's no problem. No problem at all," he says. "The more the merrier, as they say."

I nod politely, then pivot.

"Mr. Beaumont, Bex tells me you work for the defense department."

People love to talk about themselves.

"Well," he says, straightening slightly, "strictly speaking, I work with a military contractor. Not directly for the DoD."

"That must be really something, sir. Serving your country like that," I say, letting just a little awe creep into my voice. "Do you work on bombs? Rocketry? I hear there's a lot of rocket work these days."

"Well, yes, yes... it's... a good job. Solid and steady," Mr. Beaumont says, chin lifting with practiced modesty that doesn't quite hide the pomposity beneath. "I can't discuss the details, of course." He says it like it's supposed to impress. I recognize the tone. Proud of his secrets. A feeling I know a bit too well. "And how is it that you know our Beatrice?" he asks, carving another slice of roast beef, eyes flicking toward me. "Did you meet at school?"

I'm sliding a strip of beef fat into my bag when Bex jumps in. "Yes, of course. Where else would I meet him?" she blurts out. At my feet, a soft slurp echoes from the rucksack. Mr. Beaumont doesn't seem to notice. Or pretends not to. Instead, his eyes drift to Yaya, who's carefully sawing through his meal with comically delicate precision: two fingers pinching the knife, pinky up like he's at high tea. Beaumont stares, too long, with too much scrutiny.

Whack. Deborah's hand smacks his forearm, sharp and quiet. Doesn't even look at him. Mr. Beaumont blinks and redirects. He clears his throat.

"What's your field of study, Carl?"

I smile. "I'm double-majoring in forestry and wildlife management."

Bex glances over, one eyebrow lifted, a smirk pulling at her mouth. She sees I don't need saving.

"Oh, I see. Is there much money in those fields? Park rangers, is it?" Mr. Beaumont asks, feigning casual interest, but the edge in his voice gives him away. He was hoping for something respectable. Something practical. Something closer to home: doctor, lawyer, engineer maybe?

"Depends on how I use it, I suppose," I say, still smiling. "The loggers'll need new trees to replace the ones they cut down. Managing wildlife helps the hunters, the animals and their ecosystems."

"Sounds hippie dippie," he mutters.

Thunk. Deborah's foot finds his shin under the table.

"No sir," I reply calmly, "simply want to be a good caretaker to my land."

That shuts him up for a second. His brow furrows.

"Your land?"

"Yessir," I nod, slow and easy. "I'm sitting on a couple thousand acres of old-growth forest. Got a few good streams running through it. Coal mine's defunct, but—"

"H-How does a—?"

"So you can see," I cut in smoothly, "why learning how to manage it properly is important to me."

Dinner's over. Bex is inside doing dishes with her mother, voices muffled through the window. Yaya's locked himself in the guest bedroom with Squonk, probably stripped naked, airing out his balls and shedding fur like a golden retriever.

I'm out back on the porch with Mr. Beaumont. The air's brisk, but it feels almost warm compared to mountain nights. He's brought out cigars and two crystal whiskey glasses. Guess I earned a little respect when he learned I'm a landed gentleman. He pours us each a drink. Offers me a cigar.

"It'd be wasted on me, sir," I say, palms up. "But please, go ahead. I enjoy the smell."

He nods, cuts the tip with a soft snip, then sets it glowing with the practiced rhythm of a man who enjoys ceremony. I swirl the glass, sip. It's smoother than moonshine and warm in my chest. A comfortable sort of silence settles between us, for about ten seconds.

"So," he says, casual like a trigger being cocked, "what exactly are your intentions for my daughter?"

I blink. Did not anticipate that.

"W-what do you mean, sir?"

"How long have you two been dating?" he presses. "Are you going steady?"

"Uh... sir, I think there's been a bit of a misunderstanding. She, your daughter, and I are just... friends. That's all."

He scoffs, "Please. No girl brings a boy home to meet her parents if they're just friends."

I've got nothing. No sir, your daughter is helping me track down a child-murdering dragon to stop some knockoff body-snatcher apocalypse, isn't a valid response. So I just sip my drink and look out into the amber dark, letting the silence chew on us both.

"Well, sir... it warms my heart to hear that," I say, keeping it smooth. "Your daughter's quite the girl. I've fancied her for some time."

Sometimes the best yarns are built on truth. He leans back in his chair, smug as a cat in sunbeams, puffing on the cigar like he's cracked some hidden code.

"I'd like to apologize for my earlier comments," he says, waving his glass, "about your field of study. Sounds like a fine plan now that I understand the situation."

He chuckles, then sobers just enough, "I want to make sure my daughter's well taken care of. That's all. Her dream of being a writer... well, it's sweet, but it isn't going to pay any bills." He swirls his drink, then raises a brow with a grin "but none of that matters when she graduates with her MRS, am I right?" He laughs heartily at his own joke, gives my shoulder a few hearty taps.

I take another sip, slow and deep, and try not to wince.

"Your land..." Mr. Beaumont begins, swirling the last of his drink. "Are your parents well off?"

I set my glass down gently, "My parents died young. Tragic accident." I pause. "My grandfather ran the coal mine back in the day. Coal Baron Cold, they used to call him."

It sounds impressive when you say it out loud. Sounds like old money, legacy, clout. What's left unsaid is that the mine's long since dried up. The lawsuits drained what money there was. And the taxes, backed up so far, I'll be pulling schemes until I'm dead and they seize it anyhow. But you don't say that part over whiskey on a stranger's porch. Mr. Beaumont lets out a soft ah of understanding or maybe approval. He doesn't press.

"That cousin of yours," he says after a beat, nodding toward the window. "He's not going to be a problem, is he?"

I grin, just a little.

"He's a harmless dullard. Keeps to himself in a shed I built him. He's nothing to worry about." I say it just loud enough hoping the big idiot's got his ear pressed to the glass. Let him stew on that. Wanting to change the subject, I cock an eye at the pot-bellied man as he puffs on his cigar.

"So... I know you can't technically tell me anything about your work," I say, watching the smoke curl up into the porch light, "but I gotta ask. The whole Roswell thing—was it real, or just a bunch of bull roar?"

He stiffens slightly, caught between amusement and reflex. "Uhh—"

"Blink twice if aliens are real," I say, deadpan.

That gets him. He laughs, full belly, chest heaving, cigar bouncing at the corner of his mouth.

"Well," he says, shaking his head, "maybe I'll tell you after you've joined the family."

He chuckles again, clearly pleased with himself. I rise, glass in hand.

"We've got an early morning," I say, polite but final. "So I'm gonna turn in. Thank you, sir, for your hospitality. And merry Christmas."

Chapter 26
Within Talon's Reach

The morning is brisk. As we slip out, the first glow of sun begins to rise off the horizon. I pause a moment at Bex's bedroom door, but don't knock. Squonk whimpers in my rucksack, soft and guilty about leaving without a goodbye. While I rummage through the fridge and pull out a large plastic container packed with last night's leftovers, Yaya pins a note to the back of her door, folded once, neat and square

Outside, every trash can on the block has been toppled. Litter strewn across tidy lawns like confetti after a riot. A cat collar dangles impossibly in the air. "What am I gonna do with you," I mutter as I pull it from her invisible teeth. The Yow answers with an excited whine. I lift the tarp and there's a soft thud on the truck bed and the suspension groans as Snarly settles back into her place. Before shutting the tailgate, I slide her the opened plastic container. We roll out, as quiet as our rusted heap will let us.

Yaya spent the evening mapping out the child disappearances—string, pins, notes on napkins—and triangulated an active zone where the latest kids have gone missing. Now I'm behind the wheel, following his direction.

"Just so we've both got this straight," I say as we rumble down the road, "we're headed into an area where the cops are probably on high alert... to go lurk around playgrounds, looking suspicious as hell, hoping we spot a child abduction. That about right?"

"That's about the size of it," he says, unbothered.

We arrive at a playground just before sunrise. The light's weird, golden in patches, but shadowy depending on where you stand. The whole place feels half-asleep. I push Squonk on the swing as we wait. He clutches the chains with stubby fingers and lets out soft, uncertain coos. The rusted hinges creak and squeal above us like something mourning.

In the neighborhood, I spot two kids sneaking out a second-story window, bundled up tight, little hats and gloves, each with a stuffed backpack bouncing on their shoulders. I keep pushing Squonk on the swing like I didn't notice a thing. The boy and girl hit the ground running, not toward the playground, but across the street, darting into the open field beyond. Their boots crunch over the frostbitten grass, leaving a trail of tiny footprints behind them as they head toward a patch of woods in the distance. I glance back. Yaya's still behind the wheel, nose buried in his paperback like this is just another Tuesday. I keep my eyes on the sky, hand resting on Squonk's back.

"Alright, buddy," I mutter. "Let's go for a walk."

We follow the trail, slow and quiet. Once we're in the woods, it changes. The frost is gone. Everything's damp and dim, like the cold forgot to reach this far in. The root systems twist like skeletal fingers, and the tracks are harder to follow. They're half-hidden by slick leaves and jagged rock. The kids are out here somewhere. And so's whatever might be looking for them. I'm deep enough into the woods now that there's hardly any sky to watch. Gnarled branches knit overhead, blotting out the light. Then I hear it. Wings. Big ones. Flapping slow and heavy above the canopy.

I grab Squonk. He lets out a startled squoonk before diving headfirst into the rucksack with a wet splash, like a sponge falling into a puddle. I run toward the sound of wings. Breath ragged against the cold, dry air. My lungs sting. Revolver thumps in my pocket. My rifle and gear bag? Still back at the truck. I really need a better system, I think, feet pounding over roots and frozen dirt, but standing around a playground with a long gun would've drawn too much heat. I push through a thicket, branches snapping like bones around me. Something's ahead. Something big.

I break through the trees into a clearing. It's like a tornado hit a lumber yard, whole trees ripped from their roots and stacked like an enormous Lincoln Log fortress. Primitive, but sturdy. Something put real effort into this. There's more than half a dozen kids scattered around inside. The twins I followed are handing out food from their backpacks. Peanut butter and jelly, judging by the smell. Little creeps ran away from their parents to play woodland survivalists. No milk-carton kids here, they don't look abducted, more like volunteers. The twins are clearly running logistics and procurement. Efficient little operators.

I watch as children slide down from the fortress on a smooth, coiled surface, scaled, dark, and impossibly large. They laugh and giggle as they run across sprawling talons spread wide like a flower basking in sunlight. One kid's nestled in a feathered mane, trying to braid it, maybe. The tip of the tail flicks lazily in amusement. A wing, broad as a barn, lifts a small child back up onto the wall, gently like setting a bird back in its nest, so they can slide down again. I'm hunting a damned child eating monster, and instead I find Puff the

Magic Dragon. I take a step closer, toward the fortress. Every small face turns to me. Wide-eyed. Silent. I hear whispers. Low. Urgent. And above it all, the flapping of enormous wings. I raise my hands, slow and easy. Keep walking.

"Would anyone here introduce me to your large friend, please?"

An enormous serpentine tail crashes down between me and the kids—fast, hard, and mean. It slams into the earth with enough force to carve a long, arcing divot in the frozen ground. If it'd landed a foot closer, I'd be mulch. A warning. I check my pants, half expecting a warm surprise, then take a careful step back.

"Message received," I mutter, hands still raised.

Thicker than the surrounding tree trunks, the feathered serpent sits coiled on the far side of the clearing. It is silent, massive and impossibly long. I can't even guess where it begins or ends.

Its one eye, an enormous yellow orb, blinks once. Slow. Watchful. A glistening beak juts out from its scaled face, sharp enough to split bone, gleaming like polished obsidian. Talons like backhoes twitch in the frost, easily big enough to crush a car. And from its narrow back, those unfurled wings stretching like sails, blotting out the morning light.

"Squuonk?" I mutter over my shoulder. "Little help, here?"

With a rustle, Squonk plops out of the bag and into the grass at my feet. I collect myself.

"Okay," I whisper to him, eyes on the dragon. "First thing it needs to know is that the bug men are after him."

Squonk squonks up at the serpent, soft but clear.

The reaction is immediate.

Its coils rise high, feathered and tense, like a forest lifting from the ground. The clearing darkens under its shadow. The beast's head snaps toward us, fast as a striking cobra, and stops where we stood. We are saved by the gust of wind that knocked us flat. I hit the ground hard. Squonk tumbles beside me like a sack of wet towels. The thing's head looms above. Bigger than the truck. Its beak gleams black, hooked, and deadly. Underneath it, a tangle of writhing tongues undulates like eels. Its eye, a massive yellow orb, locks on me. Behind me, the tail thrashes through the air and crashes into the dirt with enough force to shake the roots loose. I scramble to my feet, legs shaking.

"They're after the Thunderbird!" I shout, desperation leaking into my voice. "We, we want to help you!" As the words leave me, I wonder how I could ever be of any help to anything this immense.

Squonk squonks with me loud and pleading. The kids join in, voices high and urgent. "Don't hurt them!" they cry, "come play!" The serpent freezes. Then slowly it pulls back, massive head retreating like a tide rolling out. Its coils loosen, its feathers flatten.

I steady my breath then ask loud and firm, "Do you know how to find the Thunderbird?"

Squonk squonks a clear, sharp reply. He knows where it roosts. The beast tilts its massive head, feathers rustling and then two jagged branches scream through the air like harpoons, tearing the quiet to pieces. They strike with thunderous force, splitting scale and muscle, sinking deep into the serpent's flank. The dragon shrieks a high, furious sound that doesn't belong to this world. The ground trembles beneath its coils as they writhe in pain, slamming into the earth like felled trees. Children scatter. Squonk screams.

I go for my gun.

"Run home!" I shout, waving the children off as they flee into the trees like startled deer. I can't see where the attack came from, not at first. A gust of wind slams into me, dropping me on my knees. Through the storm of dust and thrashing wings, I spot it. The great horned white one, Sheepsquatch.

That overgrown bastard lumbers through the trees, another rough-hewn javelin clutched in his thick, woolen fists. His goat-face locked in a snarl, like someone carved rage into driftwood and gave it horns.

"What in the hell..." I mutter. But he's not alone. Beside him, twice as massive and twice as wrong, the Grafton Monster. Naked and flopping. Slick as a river stone. No head, but two huge black eyes bulge from the flesh behind its collarbone. Its pale body pulses with muscle and wetness, like a peeled frog dipped in oil. And in the grass I spot the tops of dozens of small heads bouncing up and down through the tall grass. Their hammers raised. Not again.

My whistle cuts through the chaos, sharp and fast. The creatures are charging toward the log fort. The Snallygaster perches on top, tail flipping in a great display of force. The remaining children are huddled inside below, clutching each other in wide-eyed terror. It isn't fleeing. It's guarding them, like a broody hen ready to die for her chicks.

I run straight toward the attackers, revolver out, both hands steady. I fire into the hulking beasts as I move. The Sheepsquatch's white fur runs red but Grafton, the larger one, doesn't even flinch as a .357 slug thuds into its gut like a pebble in tar.

The squirrel-high creatures are nearly upon me now, hammers and claws brandished, bounding through the tall, dead grass like a swarm of ants out for blood.

I brace for the worst when something tears past me. A blur of fur and fang. The invisible force of nature that is the Snarly Yow hits them like a goddamn tornado. Shrieks, squeals, bones snapping. I smile and reload the spent chambers with shaking fingers. No time to celebrate. The Grafton Monster is undeterred and unbothered, marching toward the fortress like nothing in the world could stop it. I sidestep out of Snarly's chaos, and pick my target. Sheepsquatch. The white thing gone red. I rush toward it. A snub-nosed pocket revolver's useless at range, so I get close. Too close.

I squeeze off one more round before pain rips through my arm as a massive swipe sends my gun flying. I hit the ground, gasping. My arm's sliced open by that cloven bastard's blow. I'm crawling through broken grass, blood soaking into the soil, eyes locked on the gleam of my blue-steel J-frame lying just ahead. My outstretched grasping hand is skewered by a familiar needle like claw. This tommyknocker came crawling out of the grass like a damn tick. One arm's shredded; The other's pinned like a beetle in some kid's insect collection. The revolver's inches from my face. The Sheepsquatch rears up over me, towering, ready to bring my end.

A final thought slips through my mind, "at least I'm done paying taxes," but then I hear the low, rumble of my engine. The rusted heap screams into view and slams into the Sheepsquatch, ripping it away from me in a mess of fur and blood.

'Bout damn time that ape got his hands dirty. I roll onto my side, pain blinding, and tear the tommy off my arm like a leech. It hisses, needle-claws twitching. But I see my revolver glinting in the grass. I lunge, snatch it up and without thinking, swing it hard. CRACK. The steel frame smashes into the tommy's skull. Once. Twice. It drops limp in the grass like a busted marionette.

I push to my feet, with blood pooling beneath me. Not far off, I hear the groan of timber straining, the roar of the great beast, and in between, the sharp cries of children. Grafton is scaling the rough timber fortress walls, a slow unstoppable nightmare.

Then comes the crack. The Snallygaster's tail lashes out like a thunderclap. It hits Grafton hard, throwing him down in a heap. The fortress shudders. Logs shift. Support beams wail under the weight. She coils tighter, bracing for another strike. Below her, the children are screaming. The walls are buckling. The whole place is seconds from coming down.

I have to move; there's no time. The rusted truck slams to a stop, tires shrieking as they churn mud against the charging beast. The Sheepsquatch's horns punch into the hood, and the frame lurches backward, skidding several feet into what is quickly becoming a shallow bog. With a grunt, Yaya throws open the door and steps out. I sprint toward them, clutching my torn-up arm, revolver slick in my 'good' hand. Yaya meets the white monster head-on. He slams a fist straight into the snarling goat's muzzle, but the Sheepsquatch doesn't slow. It barrels into him, horns blunt and brutal, ramming his side with the force of a freight train. Yaya grunts, then roars. He grabs hold of the bleeding beast and drags it down into the muck. They twist and thrash in the cold mud, teeth and fists and fury.

I vault into the truck bed, boots slipping on the slick metal. Drop to one knee. Unzip the duffel. I pull back on the charging handle of my father's old M1 carbine and shoulder it, barrel pointing toward the wrestling beasts. Caked with mud and blood, it becomes difficult to know who's who while they struggle. I shout, "Clear!" Yaya gives a mighty kick to the beast and rolls out of the way. I dump thirty rounds of .30 caliber into Sheepsquatch's center mass. Each shot cracks like righteous thunder in my ears. It jerks and spasms and drops lifeless into the cold mud. "We're having' mutton tonight!" I shout to Yaya with a grin. The blood lust drains out of me almost as quickly as my blood. For a second I'm glad Bex wasn't here to witness this, but there's no time to breath. I shift my aim toward Grafton. It is again attempting the climb, crawling back up the fortress walls. The wood cracks and splinters beneath its weight. Inside the walls are those damned kids.

But then, the Sheepsquatch moves. It gets up. Bleeding and twitching as its grin pulls wide, tight as canvas stretched over wood. A hollow. A goddamn bugman. I drop the mag, slam a fresh one home.

"Where the fuck do the bugs stay in the host?" I shout, jumping off the truck bed.

"Try the head!" Yaya grunts, lifting the rusted heap out of deeper mud. He swings it toward the failing fortress, readying for a Hail Mary, before the whole thing collapses. I raise the rifle and take a shot. Miss. Blood loss smears my sight. I miss again. Shit. It's on top of me now. I whistle sharp and desperate. A tommyknocker flies screaming past my head, squealing midair with claws outstretched. A streak of turquoise. Good dog.

She tears into the Sheepsquatch's throat, fangs first. The Snarly Yow, fury incarnate, but the thing tosses her aside with a yelp. She bought me just enough time. CRACK. Right between the eyes. Okay, it was the left eye, but close enough. The thing crashes face-first into the mud. I stagger up and empty the rest of the mag into the back of its skull. On each trigger pull, I think of Indrid. The thought hits me harder than the recoil. All I hear is ringing, and the impotent click of the rifle with an empty mag. It doesn't get back up. Breath rattles in my chest. Mud on my boots. Blood on my sleeve. My hand still trembles. I look down at the ruin I made. A hollow puppet, sure. Maybe next time, I put the bullet in the real thing.

Maybe next time... he stays down.

Chapter 27
Suffer the Little Children

I'm woozy, crouched low in the truck bed, one shredded arm gripping the rust-pitted edge, the other clutching my rifle like a drowning man clings to driftwood. Blood seeps down the wooden stock in lazy, hot rivulets. The red of it seeps into the old grain, like it was only ever thirsty for one thing. Yaya's behind the wheel, white-knuckled and silent, driving us straight from one apocalypse into another. Giants rear up in our path, one born of folklore, the other of fever dreams. The fortress groans ahead, timbers snapping like ribs, screams of children echoing in every crack.

I can't tell how many. My vision's tunneling, a dark ring closing in. Every bump jars my bones. Every breath tastes like rust and smoke. The truck swerves hard and I slam against the side, head whipping with the turn, and that's when I see her. A flash of blond. A woman standing frozen at the edge of the woods. Eyes wide, mouth open. Bex, staring up in horror at the vast headless, naked and glistening Grafton Monster as it claws its way up the fortress walls. Looming above, wings spread wide to shield the children, is the Snallygaster. It's bloodied, breath heaving, one enormous yellow eye fixed on the coming ruin. A dragon, bracing for slaughter.

The hollows can be killed, I know that now. A clean shot to the head drops them like stones. But the Grafton Monster doesn't have a head. How the hell do I kill it with no head? Where's Squonk? My thoughts stagger. Stay awake. Stay the hell awake, Carl.

The truck slams sideways into one of the fortress supports. Wood cracks around us, timbers splintering, the frame groaning like it's about to fold in half. We've stopped. I look up, past my own bloody hands, past the edge of the truck bed, to the towering tree fort above. Sharp splinters rain down, stinging my face and eyes. Kids scream inside. I count at least three voices, maybe more.

The Snallygaster's coils rise and tremble, wounded and raging atop the groaning timbers. Her vast wings shimmer like oil slicks, talons slicing the air with blind fury. She lashes out like a rattlesnake, striking the Grafton Monster mid-climb. The serpent coils wrap tight around the slick, heaving bulk of flesh. Feathered wings beat hard against the weight, straining to lift them both. Time lurches. Holds. Then breaks. Her wings fail. They fall.

The whole forest seems to jump and the ground splits with their impact. The fort shudders and another support snaps like a dry bone. The remaining supports groan. With one arm, I start to climb. The wood is wet with blood, sap and rot. I grit my teeth and pull. A spike of pain shoots through my shoulder, then my grip gives. I fall backward, graceless and hard. My ribs scream as I hit the mud. The high-pitched, frantic cries above me sharpen, cutting through my haze, but I can't move. Fucking useless.

Before my eyes close, I see him, the yellow ape, bounding up the tower through broken beams. He leaps branch to branch, beam to beam fluid and fearless. Good monkey. My vision narrows and fades into the black.

I'm falling again, but not from the tower. The endless drop with a wine red sky above me. The sheer cliff beside me, always out of reach. A sea of souls stretch out before me like the end of everything. I fall forever, but never seem any closer. I turn my attention away from the doom that waits for me. There it is floating above me, black against the sky, enormous as God. Its wings spread like the veil of night. It watches and waits. I reach toward the black vision filling my sight.

I'm in the cold thick mud and grass. There's something warm and wet covering me. Soothing gurgles ripple all around me. A viscous fluid becomes a soft and pliable membrane, pulsing against my chest. Forcing my heart to pump. My quiet companion, my oldest friend, now a blood brother. He flows in my veins, his strength is now mine. I sit up sharp and sudden, with a wet shhlrp as I pull myself out of the mud. Squonk's membrane extends out to my slashed arm, sealing the wound.

The world is chaos. Timbers crack. Screams echo. Feathers drift through the air like dying leaves. I grab my rifle from the mud and I climb. Yaya's halfway down the tower with three kids clinging to his body like baby possums, suspended from his arms and wrapped around his thick legs. His grip is iron, but his face is tight. This is taking everything he's got.

To my surprise, Bex is above scrambling across the crumbling timbers, one child in her arms, another a few feet back. He's frozen stiff, rooted in panic. She's shouting, pleading, trying to get him to move. The roof groans, and another support gives. It's coming down.

Across the clearing, the Snallygaster is wrapped tight in a death hold. Grafton's slick muscled arms squeeze and crush her midsection. The beast thrashes, wings slicing air, talons carving the earth, but it's no use. Her strength is failing. Her great body sags, coiled too tight to breathe. She's losing. I reach Yaya on the descent.

"Two more up there," he barks between breaths, nodding toward Bex. "The older's not moving."

I look up and see the girl in her arms, see the boy behind her. Frozen. Terrified. She made the hard choice, climbing down with the young girl, leaving the petrified boy to die. I climb faster. Squonk is with me, in and around me. His fear, his courage, all tangled up with my own. I can feel the children's panic. The roar of the Grafton Monster. The strain in Bex's chest as she descends. I feel everyone. Everyone... but one. The Snallygaster's light is fading.

Yaya shouts up to me, "It don't got a head!"

"It's got eyes," I mutter as I continue the climb. A large cracking sound erupts like the sky broke in half. The roof collapses above us. Logs crack and slide, slamming into each other and tumbling through the air.

One bounces off a beam above me and wedges itself blocking my path. Another crashes beside Bex, throwing splinters into her coat. Somehow, she's still holding on, but the kid in her arms is writhing and screaming. Full-body panic. The kid's flailing limbs keep Bex from getting any leverage. She's pinned, twisted against the crumbling structure, no way to climb down. The other child must be crushed or buried. I don't let myself think too long on it. I reach her. Arms shaking. Heart full.

"I got you," I say, breath rough, and wedge my knee into a groove in the broken wood beside her. I use my frame to bear their weight and give Bex's arms a second of relief. She gasps, clutches me tight. The girl between us is still panicked, hyperventilating. Then, Squonk, I don't know how, but I feel him radiating warmth, calm, and safety. The girl softens in my arms, sobbing quiet. I cradle her close.

"What's your name, darlin'?" I ask her gently, lips near her ear.

"M-Marie Sue."

"Well, Marie Sue, everything's gonna be alright. You're gonna go with Miss Bex here, and she's gonna get you down safe. I'm gonna go up and check on your friend, alright?"

She nods. Little tears still caught in her lashes.

"T-thank you," she stammers.

Bex is trembling beside me, her face streaked with grime and tears. When she presses into me to take the girl, I feel her heart hammering. There's more there. Something I see in her eyes, in her breath on my neck. Something unsaid, but loud as a scream. I don't say anything.

"Okay, Bex. I need to get up there. You good?"

She nods, scared and brave.

"Good," I say, "go."

She starts down, slower now with the girl in her arms, but steady. Squonk burns in my chest like a second heartbeat, giving me the strength I need to last just a little longer. I turn back to the climb, rifle across my back, blood crusted down my side. The top of the fort is a ruin. Splintered timbers. Crushed logs. A platform barely holding on above the death below. A log jam in the sky. And someone's still under it.

"Hello!? Hello!?" I shout into the wreckage, searching, begging. No answer. Just splinters, smoke, and stillness. Below me, the battle nears its brutal end. Two gods battling in a graveyard of trees. Snallygaster's coils are limp now, body battered and crushed. Grafton looms over it like an executioner.

The Sheepsquatch went down with a well placed shot to the eye. That did the trick. This one's a much bigger target. I swing the rifle off my back, charge it, and set my sights. My body is wrecked. Arms shaking. One eye swollen nearly shut. Doesn't matter. I squeeze the trigger. CRACK. The shot echoes like a hammer on steel. The Grafton Monster reels back. It falters. Its grip on the serpent loosens. I squeeze again. CRACK. Hot metal whistles through the air. The bullet punches through its massive black eye nestled behind its enormous collarbone. Wet, violent. The slick flopping giant flails. Its whole body shudders like a wave hitting rock, and then it stills. Snallygaster coils tight, and with a final, vengeful crack of its tail, slams the monster into the ground. The earth shakes, and something inside me shakes with it.

Logs shift and I see it. A small hand. Pale. Barely moving. Pinned beneath a pile of timber.

"HELP! Help me!" I scream. I don't care who hears. I need someone. No answer. I throw myself toward the collapsed logs, hearts pounding. I wedge my shoulder under the first one. The bark bites into my back. My legs tremble with the strain. I push. I scream. I swear. I curse the trees, the gods, the mountain. Nothing budges.

"Come on—come on!" I growl through my teeth. I try again. I will these trees to move. The boy is still alive under there and he isn't going to die alone. Swift as a cobra, the feathered serpent thrusts upward, rising above me like smoke off a battlefield.

"Help me, please!" I beg. The kid's life is bleeding away through the cracks, and I've got nothing left but pleading. The serpent watches me with its massive yellow eye locked on me. I see something in it. She isn't some feral animal. She's as old as time and worn with grief. She understands. A great weight stirs in my chest, like sorrow passed down through generations, too big for one soul to carry. A god with no home, no kin, no sky to rule. The pain of a thing that's only ever been misunderstood. Its wings beat overhead. Talons like excavators plunge into the mess of logs, lifting and clearing them aside with terrifying ease. Splintered timber tossed like twigs. And beneath the ruin, there he is.

The boy, bloodied and bent in ways bodies ought not to be, but still some breath left in his chest. I stagger forward and fall to my knees beside him. "Squonk, keep him safe," I whisper, patting the membrane across my chest. I feel my second heartbeat slow and then stop. With a tug and a pull, one soul peels off from another, and I hear the rushing of wind as I fall into a reddened sky.

Chapter 28
Friends in Low Places

The black bird mocks me with its stillness as I fall through eternity toward the sea of souls. The sky burning red at the edges where its wings touch the horizon.

"Mr. Bellinghausen, sir? How are we feeling today?"

How are we feeling? Like turkey-basted roadkill.

"Oh, I'm doing great, thank you kindly. Ready to get on out of here," I say, flashing a grin that feels like borrowed teeth.

"Sir, I think you'll be with us a few more days at least. You were in quite the state when your wife brought you in. The surgeon had a heck of a time with that arm. We went through a lot of blood bags yesterday. We just want to make sure there's no risk of infection. A bear, was it?"

"Is my wife here? I'd like to see her."

I'm laying in a hospital bed. Naked under a blue gown. My left arm's wrapped tight in gauze and held in a splint. Tubes in my nose. Tube in my arm. Tube in my dick. My right hand, lightly bandaged, is cuffed to the bed rail like I might bolt at any second. Cute.

"I'm afraid she just stepped out. Something about a monkey's uncle."

"That's fine," I say. "Just fine."

"There are some other fellas want a word with you, though."

Fuck, here we go. There's a quick tap at the hospital room door. Just a courtesy knock, not a request. Two stiffs walk in. Dapper. Like mannequins dressed for a funeral. Black suits, black hats. Pale as raw dough. Sunglasses indoors, of course. They move... oddly. Rigid, like their joints only bend one way. Like someone explained walking to them in theory and they've just about got the hang of it. For a moment, I brace expecting bugmen, but no. The faces aren't right. These men wear scowls, not smiles.

"Hello, gentlemen. What can I do for you?" I ask, sweet as sugar, innocent as the day I was born.

"Is your name Fabian Bellingshausen?" one of them asks, his voice all angles and iron.

"Fabian Gottlieb von Bellingshausen," I reply, thickening my accent into a cartoon German before dropping it like a bad joke. Gotta amuse myself somehow. The nurse takes the cue and slips out, leaving me alone with the suits and my catheter.

"What were you doing in that park yesterday morning?"

"My morning jog."

"This will go much smoother if you do not lie to us, Mr. Bellingshausen."

I pause, just a beat.

"Is the boy okay?" I ask. Can't help it. The question slips out before I can measure it. One of the suits stiffens, jaw tight. Bad cop, I wager.

The other softens just a hair, "He will live, multiple compound fractures. Concussion. He'll be fine with proper treatment and time."

Ah, Good Cop.

Bad Cop starts up again, "Did you enter into mutual combat with a creature known as the Sheepsquatch?"

"The nurse said it was a bear," I reply, laying it on thick. Maybe if I play dumb long enough, they'll tire out.

"We've matched your fingerprints," Good Cop says. "Ballistics off your rifle and revolver. You shot the creature no less than sixty times."

"Is that right?"

"Yes. It is."

"So am I under arrest? Gonna read me my rights? I hear that's a thing now."

"We aren't law enforcement," Good Cop says smoothly.

Bad Cop turns toward him like a mannequin rotating on an invisible base. The air in the room shifts. Colder now.

"We work for an organization outside your law. Outside your government," he says, voice low and clinical. "We clean up the kinds of messes that would fracture your pathetic little minds."

I stare at them both for a second. He steps closer, the shadows on his face refusing to move naturally. Almost like they're glued there. He pulls a dark, hard edged electronic device from his pocket. With a flick of his thumb, the device beeps. With every step he takes toward me the beeping gets faster, louder even. He turns to Good Cop and nods, "The radiation signatures match with the other invasive species." With a flourish, he flicks the device off and drops it back into his coat pocket. Good Cop whispers quite low, "That can't be the case... Humans don't—"

Bad Cop interrupts him by continuing my interrogation, "What is your relationship," he says evenly, "to the Blemmye known as the Grafton Monster?"

"I have no idea what you're talking about," I say flatly.

"You shot it no less than seven times," Good Cop says.

"If you say so."

"I do." Bad Cop steps forward again, voice like a blade. "Where is Quetzalcoatl?"

"The what now?"

"Níðhöggr, then. Where is she?" Bad Cop demands.

"Gesundheit,"

"The serpent," Good Cop clarifies, "also known colloquially as the Snallygaster; According to witness accounts, you interfered on her behalf."

I shrug. "I have no idea."

I pause, eyeing them both. "Are those latex masks? Creepy as all get-out."

"You don't like them?" Good Cop asks with surprise in his voice.

"What are you?" I ask, tilting my head. "Reptilians? I've never met Reptilians before."

Bad Cop hisses, sharp and low. "We're asking the questions."

"Relax," I say. "I've got a ton of questions too. Are you aliens? A civilization older than humans? Or both?"

The eager one looks like he's about to spill something, but the mean one shuts it down with a glance. Good Cop must be a trainee, the poor bastard. I like him.

"The creature known as the Grafton Monster has been disposed of," Bad Cop says, cold and flat. "No one will know it ever existed."

"So," I say, eyebrow raised, "you're not leaving any witnesses?"

"Oh, no—nothing like that!" Good Cop blurts, waving his hands like he's shooing a fly.

Bad Cop shoots him another glare. The dread he's trying to wrap me in keeps slipping off like a cheap blanket.

"What did you do to those children, then?" I ask.

"Why, hypnotized them!" Good Cop says, far too cheerfully.

Bad Cop doesn't flinch. "We also implanted a post-hypnotic suggestion. If you try to expose what happened—papers, television, law enforcement—we'll activate it."

"Meaning what, exactly?" I ask, voice low.

"They'll see your face," he says, voice like ice, "and call you the bad man."

I go quiet for a moment, "There's no need for these threats."

"Then answer our questions," Bad Cop says firmly.

I sigh, long and low. "Alright... Shoot."

Good Cop steps back, shuts the door with a soft click. Bad Cop asks, "Are you, or are you not, Carlisle Boone Cold?" I feel it then, that twist in the gut. That name doesn't get bounced around much, especially not by strangers. Good Cop interjects "We don't care about the medical fraud. We've seen the pattern. Different names, same story. Half-dead and full of holes. Get patched up. Disappear. Always just a few paces ahead of where our division ends up getting dispatched."

I swallow, "Yeah. Yes... Folks call me Carl. Cryptid Carl, to my clientele."

Bad Cop doesn't blink, "Are you, or are you not, the spawn of Indrid Cold, also known as the Smiling Man?"

The room feels smaller all of a sudden.

"He was a bastard in life," I say, voice like gravel, "he's a monster in death."

Bad Cop folds his hands behind his back, stiff as a corpse. "Have you, or have you not, been aiding varieties of extinct and invasive species across the Appalachian range for the last three years?"

I stare at the ceiling tiles a long moment, counting the stains.

"Longer," I say, "but yeah, last three've been my vocation, of sorts."

Good Cop perks up like a hound catching a scent. "Seems like we're in the same line of work," he says, chipper like we just discovered we shop at the same feed store.

Bad Cop doesn't flinch, "Where is the... Snallygaster?"

I blink slow, "What, she a cousin or somethin'?"

His jaw tightens, "Had you not confirmed your identity, we'd have wiped you clean. Hypnosis. Neural flush. Scrub every unusual event from your memory."

I shrug, "Might take a while."

He leans in, "Where is the Snallygaster?"

I hold his stare, even through the tint of those bug-eyed glasses.

"Safe, I hope," I say. "I don't know. Don't know what happened after Grafton fell."

Good Cop steps closer, tilting his head like he's just remembered something personal.

"I pulled up your records," he says, "your land, the mountain, are you using it as an animal preserve? Strange weather patterns up there."

I nod slow. Feeling naked and gutted on the slab. "They don't call it Storm Mountain for nothin'," I add.

Bad Cop clicks his tongue, "Seems like you've had a hell of a time holding on to it. What happens when you fall behind on your payments, Mr. Cold?"

Good Cop smirks, "We'd have a lot more work around here, that's for sure. He's privatizing our public works. The higher ups are always looking for cost savings. Would be a real shame if that ended."

I don't rise to the bait.

Bad Cop cuts through the moment. "When is the last time you encountered Indrid Cold?"

"Flatwoods," I say, "about a month back."

Good Cop stiffens a little, "There were some reports from that region a while ago, but it went quiet. We didn't follow up."

"It went dead quiet," I tell him. "Doubt there's a soul left."

Good Cop blinks behind the lenses, "We were not aware of that. Thank you for your cooperation, Mr. Cold. We'll follow up."

He then unshackles me from the bed. Bad Cop steps toward the door. "Stay quiet. Stay healthy. I hope we don't meet again."

They turn and I watch them go. Bad Cop is the first to exit, and just before the Good Cop leaves, I lift my hand and mouth the word: "Where?" Then I flip my finger to the sky, then earth. Good Cop hesitates. The rubbery face doesn't move, but behind the lenses, his eyes flicker. And then, he points down.

Bex walks in with her arms full. A bouquet in one hand, a box of donuts in the other. "Look who finally decided to come back to the living," she says. "Who are the suits?"

"Reptilians from the Hollow Earth," I reply, voice dry as dust. "Come to check up on me. What can I say, I've got friends in low places."

She scoffs. "You got your humor back, I see." She moves to the little table by the window and starts arranging the bouquet, mums, marigolds, black-eyed Susans. All colors of fire. Autumn in a vase.

"I got you the manliest bouquet in the shop," she says, straight-faced. "At least, that's what the florist told me."

"Well," I say, settling back into the scratchy hospital pillow, "I'm just happy to have such a doting wife, Mrs. Bellingshausen."

She sits beside the bed, shifting awkwardly in the hard chair, her eyes warm. "It was the only way they'd let me see you," she says. "Yaya chose the name."

"Course he did. Is everyone... alright?" I ask, the question and it sits heavier on me than I expected.

"All but you," she says softly.

"I'll be fine," I grunt, shifting in the bed, "soon as they take this tube outta my prick."

A dry grin pulls at her lips. She tries not to laugh, but I catch the twitch in her cheek.

"You almost weren't," she says, voice tight.

I eye my rucksack sitting in the corner where she dropped it. A soft, gurgled coo rises from inside. After a moment's squirming effort, the Squonk wriggles free and crawls up the side of the bed like a slug with purpose. He settles at my feet with a contented sigh, warm and solid. I nod, let the silence settle for a second before asking, "Where's Snally?"

"The mountain," she says. "Yaya and Squonk... talked it down. Somehow. He's got some sort of history with it, I guess." She hesitates, eyes flicking to the window like she might spot feathers on the skyline.

"He flew off on it."

Showoff.

"Where's Snarly?" I ask.

"In the back of the truck," Bex says with a sigh, "She doesn't like me driving it."

"She hurt ya?"

"Not yet." She eyes the scar on my cheek, the one part of me that doesn't need healing.

"I'll talk to her," I mutter. "She's a jealous bitch."

"Did she eat my neighbor's cat?"

"Who's to say?"

We chuckle at that, and the room goes quiet.

"Did I ruin your Christmas?" I ask.

"Hardly," she scoffs. "You met my folks. I'd rather fight giants."

I sigh, reach over, and place my hand on hers. It's warm, and soft. "They ain't perfect" I say. ", but love 'em while you got 'em. Not after."

That quiet settles in again. Heavy with everything unsaid. Then I clear my throat. "Well, my beautiful wife is here to help me use the toilet, so let's get these tubes outta me."

I press the call button.

PART 4:
CATCHING COLD

Chapter 29
The Missing God

Well, it's a cold one. January's teeth are sunk deep into everything. Cold down to the bone, cold in the thoughts, cold in the silence that fills up every corner of this busted trailer we call home. Even the fire feels tired. The potbelly stove tries its best, but the heat slips through the walls like it don't care to stay. Can't say I blame it.

Bex is gone again. Back at school up north. Told her I'd be fine, and maybe I even meant it. Now, I sit with Yaya across from me, flipping through his dog-eared paperback in the dark like he's trying to finish it before the end of the world. Squonk's curled up in my lap like a whimpering little hot water bottle. The invisible weighted blanket that is the Snarly Yow, lays across my feet and snores like a demon with sinus issues. Her size pushes me further from the stove's fire light than I like, but the furnace inside her shaggy fur lined chest, might be the only reason why I've made it through the last several winters.

Bex and I bailed from the hospital on day four. I wasn't built for places that smell like antiseptic and piss. They said I'd need months to heal, maybe longer. Joke's on them, I don't have months. Took the splint off myself. Arm still works, more or less. Hurts like hell, but I'll take pain over uselessness any day. Still haven't gotten my guns back. Reptilians kept those, I guess. Probably for evidence. Or a souvenir. Either way, I'm light on steel and lighter on money. I'm sure my PO box is full to the brim with threats.

Ain't had much in the way of sun these days, and the hens ain't laying. Tried getting work from the old Dutch folks down the way, but they took one look at my busted arm and sent me packing. Kind about it, though. Gave me some bread, some meat, and a moth eaten sweater. They've always been good to me over the years, even when they cast me out for consorting with devilry.

Squonk assures me the Snallygaster knows where the Thunderbird roosts. All that madness to keep a secret, so of course, I asked her to take me to it. It was a shorter trip than I expected. She scooped me up with a gentleness that I wouldn't expect from an eldritch creature with talons that remind me of Vlad the Impaler. She, the feathered one-eyed serpent with tentacle tongues, carried me up into the crackling clouds that swirl around my mountain and placed me upon the summit. The storm seems more alive up there. It is disorienting to be at eye level with the clouds full of lightning. There was an odd hum beneath the blowing wind, like it knew my name. But there weren't no bird up there, I'm starting to think the Snally is a bit touched. Or maybe I am, who's to say?

I expected Indrid to figure out where we'd be, it was his mountain first, after all. Expected him to come with some grand entrance, for him to take back what's his. But he didn't. My guess? Weather. No army should try and invade Russia during winter. Doubt this is any different, 'cept its a steep climb. Doubt even his monsters would do well in a whiteout blizzard when it's twenty below.

So I wait. Fire crackles. The ape turns pages. Squonk snores. I sit in the hush and stare into the orange guts of that stove across the room like it's gonna tell me something. On the radio, the obituaries are read aloud. More than usual. Is he building an army? Breathe slow. Deliberate. Waiting. Thinking. The heat dances across my face in flickers and pulse. My eyes close, and I drift, pulled under by a familiar wave. The insides of my eyelids glow, red and pulsing. And for the first time in weeks, I feel warm. Not warm, hot. Muggy. The kind of heat that clings to your skin like a second breath.

I open my eyes slow, like waking from a dream. The trailer is gone. The fire. The folding chair. My companions are gone too. I'm sitting naked on the ground, bare against the frozen soil of my own mountain. Only it's not frozen anymore. The sky has turned a vivid, bleeding red. The storm still coils around the summit, lightning sizzling through the haze. And there, towering above me like the Statue of Liberty standing atop Everest, a massive black figure. Hooked beak. Feathered wings stretched like nightfall.

I'm shaken back into the freezing trailer with the dim crackle of fire in the iron belly of the stove. Yaya's hand rests on my shoulder. He smiles, says he's goin' to bed. I grumble, slow to leave the warmth of the dream. "I must've been... saw the bird."

"Then it's on the other side." Yaya shrugs.

I scoop up Squonk from my lap and hand him over. He melts into the ape's arms without protest, curling into a ball like dough in a bread bowl. Yaya nods once and disappears into the dark of the bunk room.

I turn to Ol' Snarly. She's still heavy across my feet, but her ears twitch as I rub along the thick ridge of her neck. I find the spot behind her ear and scratch. She moans low, then nudges her massive head against my thigh like she missed me. "Time to go outside," I whisper, pushing up from the chair. She yawns, a cavernous sound, and rises slow, her joints popping like the logs in the stove. We head for the door. I feel her shift beneath the stillness, alert and ready. I zip up my hoodie, pull my gloves tight, and we step out into the cold.

Chapter 30
The Womb of the Abyss

Under the light of constellations, the dark shaggy dog might be mistaken for a moose. I let her lead the way. Each step sizzles and boils the snow beneath her feet, clearing the path to the rock face. With only a vague notion of where the eyeless woman disappeared, I run my gloved hand across the rock wall. I grew up here. I've been dedicate, or damned, to this rock my whole life. I thought I knew its secrets, but a blind woman found something I never knew and slipped away without a sound. I walk along the wall, gliding my numb fingers across the frozen stone. The pain of my mangled arm shoots sparks across my mind, until I find it again. Her crevice, impossible to see, unless you know how to look. I couldn't tell you why I'm compelled to enter.

I leave Snarly bathing in a now steaming snowbank. The further I slip inside the rock, the less grip the cold has on me. A welcome escape from the ice. An escape into another world, a silent world. It's narrow and twisting. I walk forward. My awareness of the bulk and heat of my layers increases with time. I strip down, one layer after the other scattered along the floor of the narrowing passage. I'm crawling on hands and knees, the ceiling pressed hard against my back. My flashlight, the last of my possessions clenched between my teeth. The air changes. I slip through the narrow blackness into an open void. I have no sense of enclosure here. It's as if I walked outside and the sun, moon and stars all blinked out of existence at once. I can only feel the cool stone floor on my bare feet. I stop and listen. I hear a faint trickle from an unknowable distance. I cautiously step toward the direction of the sound when an impossibly dark silhouette stands in front of me. My eyes don't work here, but somehow I see her all the same. Her long fingers intertwine with my own, and her cloaked figure presses into me. She must have worked the stiff leather rigorously since her disappearance, because it feels soft and supple against my skin. My awareness seems to open with her touch. This void is a cathedral carved by time. A thin waterfall spills from the ceiling in a silver thread, feeding a stream that winds through the cavern floor. Its path etched over centuries of defiance. A low hum vibrates in the rock. The bones of the earth still sing.

I lift my flashlight. The yellow beam cuts across the dark like a blade, carving shadows into the walls, sweeping across the stone... And then it lands on her. Miss Sally. Her skin glows beneath the light, translucent as creek water, thin as a jellyfish veil. I see everything beneath. Soft muscle shifting. Hard ribs rising. Her lungs expand with slow reverence, like breath itself is a prayer. Behind her breasts, her heart thuds steady—a war drum in the deep dark. Her veins run like river maps beneath glass. Quiet. Winding. Endless. She shows no signs of age. She's ancient and endless. Something sacred. With a click, I turn off the light.

She says nothing. Still holding my one hand full of fire, she uses her other to build a topographical map in her mind. Her hand moves with purpose, searching down me with care. She guides me to settle onto a stone ledge worn into the shape of something like a bed. She wraps the patchwork cloak around us both, and we sit. Only the stream murmurs. The waterfall whispers. And somewhere beneath it all, a smoldering drone hums low and deep.

"The tunnels must connect to the old mine, somehow", I think to myself.

She rests against me; small and warm. Her breath brushes my chest. I wrap the cloak tighter around us both, and we sit in the silence.Her delicate heart flutters against me. The world fades, its edges gone soft and distant. There's nothing left here but her warmth against my ribs. The deep dark of the cave around us disappears into an inky endless void. I hold her and let the abyss take me. My eyes, or maybe my mind, fill with color. Shapes twist and spiral. Swirling paths, radiant and strange, unfurl before me like roots through time.

Is this what she sees? Is this how she moves through the world? Each path pulses with promise. I could fall into any of them just by wishing it so, but her hand grips me by my root and anchors me into this empty realm, Ginnungagap. She's behind me now, pressing close, her bare form curled into my spine. She turns my face with the other hand. Our mouths meet and fractals explode across my mind like fireworks behind a kaleidoscope. She slides into my lap with alien grace. Moves like water. Like wind through grass. She lowers herself onto me—slow, certain—and her breath catches as her body wraps around mine. Her long hair brushes my face. I hold her close. And for the first time, I see and know her, Auðumbla. The woman between worlds. Older than the mountains that rose and fell around her. Forgotten in the seams of time. Lost in the cracks of reality. A soul who can only exist in forgotten places, in quiet shadows where time forgets to look. My goddess of the gaps. Her hips roll like the tide of some great sea. We move together, fuse together, until there's no separation. No edges. No breath of space between us. Her form bursts in color, a spectrum, a scream and then: White.

A moment that blooms and dies all at once. The visions fade like steam on stone. She lies atop me now, weightless as mist, breath quiet in the crook of my neck. My hand rests against the curve of her back beneath the cloak. I listen to the slow, eternal trickle of falling water, a lullaby written in stone.

Chapter 31
No Room for Silence

The summit cuts through the sky like a broken tooth, and I sit there, cross-legged and cold, feeling like the world's biggest dumbass. Wind whips across the peak, slicing through every layer I've got on, tugging at my sleeves, howling down my neck like the mountain's trying to talk me out of whatever foolishness I'm about to do. I breathe deep. Then again. Then once more, trying to calm the itch in my bones, the noise in my head. I close my eyes.

Nothing. No veil pulling back. No secret knowledge seeping in through the cracks. Just the hiss of wind and the throb of my knees on cold stone.

"You're too angry," Yaya had said, flipping through his dog-eared paperback like it held the answers. "Can't pass between when you're full of fire, it won't take you."

I had a bitter laugh at that. Told him maybe the fire's what I need to get through, but truth is, I didn't believe him. Not then. I'd been raised on this mountain. Born here. First breath in the high air. My blood's in the soil, my memories tangled in its roots. I know these woods better than I know my own scarred face. If anyone should be able to slip through its wounds, it's me. But now? I feel like a fool. The wind mocks me, tugging at my hood like a scolding mother. The cold finds every crack in my resolve.

"Used to be easier," Yaya told me over a cup of that bitter chicory tea. "Before the power lines. Before all the noise. We used to walk between like stepping through fog. But now? The wires hum, and the towers scream, and the veil thickens."

He looked at me with those tired eyes. The kind of tired that sees more than it lets on.

"But you," he said. "You're of the mountain where the veil is mighty thin. Might be it's still open to you. Might be it remembers."

And here I am. Trying to force a door that won't budge. I sit still, try to clear my head, but Bex's face keeps floating up behind my eyelids. Her laughter, her fire, the way she looked at me after my stint at the hospital, like I mattered. Like I wasn't just some wounded mutt.

Then there's Indrid. His smug grin. The way he smiles like he knows how it all ends. The carrion husks he's left behind in the wake of whatever plan he's working. The eyes of those children. The loss in Snallygaster's voice. The bone-deep fear I haven't been able to shake since Flatwoods. I try to push it all down. Try to empty my mind like Yaya said. But it just keeps filling back up with ghosts and hate.

I don't know how long I sit there. Long enough for my fingers to go numb. Long enough for the storm clouds to gather again. Eventually, I give up. I stand, bones stiff and look out across the forest. Snow-dusted branches sway below, a patchwork of ash and pine. Somewhere down there, Indrid Cold is moving pieces on a board I can't even see. And I'm here, sitting with a thumb up my frozen ass. Meditating like some cult dropout.

"Enough," I mutter. I don't have time to wait for visions or spirit quests. Don't have the patience for sacred wisdom or humming crystals or whatever the hell's supposed to happen up here. If the veil wants me, it knows where I am. But until then? I've got a cryptid to hunt. I stomp back down the trail, boots crunching in the snow, breath like smoke pouring from my mouth. The cold doesn't bite the same way now. Anger's warming me just fine. Yaya's sitting outside the trailer when I get back, wrapped in blankets, steam rising from a tin mug. He watches me without a word.

"Didn't work," I say flatly.

He nods once, as if he expected it.

"I ain't waiting for him," I say.

"You going after him?"

"I am."

There's a long pause. The only sound is the wheeze of the old stove pipe and the slow drip of snowmelt off the awning.

"He'll see you coming," Yaya says.

"Good."

"You might not come back."

"I might not."

Squonk peeks his head out of the trailer, blinking like he's been napping through the end of the world. He squeaks softly, waddles to my side.

"You comin'?" I ask him.

He squonks once. That's all I need. I throw my gear together. The shotgun. Some shells. My last clean shirt. Not much else to bring. Yaya doesn't try to stop me.

"The new radio equipment I installed in the truck last week, make sure ya keep it tuned where it is, I'll keep you updated." He says solemnly without a goodbye.

The engine growls to life beneath me, and the rusted torn up heap rumbles down the mountain road, with a new tall and swaying antenna, like it knows where we're going. I'm done waiting on him.

It's time to catch a Cold.

Chapter 32
The Empty Road

I've been drifting down these narrow, winding country roads for the better part of a week now. One dying town to the next. Empty streets. Hollowed out storefronts. A whole country of ghosts, and not a soul left to notice.

Squonk's curled up in my lap, mashing his face against the driver's side window, leaving greasy little smudges with every breath. My shotgun, the last gun I got, sits in the rack behind my head. The truck heater clicks and wheezes, but it still throws enough warmth to keep the frost off my knuckles. Better than waiting to die on the mountain, frozen solid with regret.

Yaya's on the radio, some jerry-rigged walkie-ham-antenna thing he cobbled together. I don't understand it, but it works. He's guiding me from one ghost town to the next. Hunting whispers. I miss Ol' Snarly. Hell of a comfort, that dog. But she's the best line of defense I've got, and if the horde comes, Yaya's gonna need her more than I do. The Snallygaster, she ain't been the same since she came to the mountain. She's listless and withdrawn, like she's grieving. A mother without her children. She hides out most days, buried in a pile of felled logs.

I pull up to an old dilapidated gas station leaning like it's tired of standing. Place looks like it hasn't seen a customer in weeks. The convenience store is dark inside. Dingy and quiet. No hum of refrigeration. No clerk behind the counter. Just dust and the stale smell of motor oil and rot. I grab a few packs of jerky off the shelf, something sweet for Squonk. Then I slide behind the counter and pop the till. Not much in there, but it all goes into the rucksack just the same. Coins, crumpled bills, a faded lottery ticket someone once believed in.

Outside, I thumb the pump on and let the truck drink deep. It's been thirsty a while. Since I got deep into these sticks, I've barely seen a soul. Just shuttered windows and forgotten places. I've got enough gold for wolves, sure, but it don't feel like I'm any closer to finding Indrid. Just more silence and more road.

I point the truck east and head for Mecklenburg. Far enough out that it oughta be untouched. I haven't been back since before Flatwoods. Before everything went sideways. The drive's long and groggy. The winter sun is a smear on the windshield. Squonk sleeps most of the way, curled up like a dog with dreams too big for his body. We roll into town just before dusk. I pull into the old bank lot and kill the engine.

I shuffle through the wad of loose cash I've scraped together and sort it slow. A heavy lump of change goes in my last clean sock. Who knows where the other one is? I stuff it into my hoodie pocket and get to stacking bills. It's dumb, but there's a comfort in counting. In having something solid in hand.

And it's good to see people again. Real people. Moving. Laughing. Faces in windows, boots on sidewalks. After all the empty husks I've wandered through, this place feels almost... alive. But then, something itches at the corners of my vision. Passersby. Just shadows at first. Glimpses. Too smooth. Too synced. I blink hard, tell myself

I'm just anxious. Just tired. There's nothing odd here. Not anymore. Not since we relocated Mortimer.

I leave Squonk curled up in the truck, snoring like a busted air hose. Grab my rucksack and head for the bank, hoodie pocket heavy with sock change. The front door gives a tired chime as I step inside. Place smells like air freshener and printer toner. Quiet. Only one teller behind the counter. She's turned away, focused on something I can't see.

I put on my best smile, plastic as a fake ID.

"Good afternoon," I say, cheerful as can be. "I'd like to exchange some cash for a cashier's check."

She doesn't turn right away. Just stills for a second too long, then slowly pivots in her chair.

"Yes sir," she says, voice honey-thick. "We'd love to help you, but..."

Her face hits me like a bucket of cold grease. Eyes black as oil slicks. Grin too wide, too stiff, like her skin's trying to remember how to wear a face. She rises.

"We seem to have some trouble with your account," she says, smoothing her skirt like it matters. "The mayor would like to have a word with you."

The mayor steps out from the back, silhouette all shoulders and slicked hair. But that politician's grin is gone now, peeled back into something stretched and wrong. The glad-handing mask has slipped, and what's underneath is nothing but meat and menace. Bony claws where handshaking fingers used to be. Eyes like empty wells.

A flash of anger hits me, sharp and stupid, for walking in here unarmed. But showing up to a bank with a shotgun and a sack tends to raise the wrong kind of flags. He lunges. I dodge just enough, but not clean. His claws rip the strap from my shoulder, wrenching the rucksack free as I stumble toward the exit. Shit.

"I believe this belongs to me, young man," he growls, clutching the bag like it's a prize hog at the fair.

My good hand is already in my hoodie pocket. Fingers close around the ankle of my sock—full of silver, copper and nickel and every hard-earned sin I could scrounge. I pull it free, let the weight drop, the coin-laden end hangs heavy toward the floor.

"Don't forget your change!" I shout and swing. The sock cracks across his grinning face with a solid thunk, bursting like a cheap piñata. Quarters and dimes spray across the lobby, bouncing off tile and teeth alike. The mayor reels back, clawed hands flailing, more shocked than hurt. It's enough. I snatch the bag and bolt for the door, heart in my throat. I hit the sunlight and then—

Wham. The ground punches the air out of me as I'm slammed face-first into the asphalt. Two uniforms pin me down, all knees, elbows and radio static. One of them's barking something in a tone that's too calm to be helpful. My cheek's grinding into the blacktop. I can't see much past boot soles and blurry sky.

"Well," I grunt, "that could've gone smoother."

Chapter 33
Prodigal Bound

I'm sitting in a small, ancient holding cell, stone walls and iron bars, built sometime before the country was even an idea. The kind of place where justice smells like mildew and regret. I wonder, not for the first time, if this is where they locked up John Brown after his raid. Seems the sort of place that holds onto old ghosts. I'm being held by the local law. Not bad men, maybe. But bad enough to serve a mayor who isn't corrupt so much as corrupted. A hollow. A bugman. And if the mayor's turned... how many more? I stare through the bars and count shadows. I don't know who's still human in this place, but I doubt I will be for long.

They've likely towed the truck by now. My shotgun was inside, the last real weapon I had. Don't know if Squonk's in it... or if he bailed. Hard to picture him staying put with sirens wailing. He's smart and sensitive. Might've slipped off into the woods or into someone's tool shed by now, sobbing and scared. I don't know much of anything right now. Assault on a mayor. Attempted bank robbery. Hell, they could pin half the damn town's problems on me if they wanted to. Maybe they will.

There's no phone call. No rights read. No lawyer with his tie half-knotted trying to play savior. Just silence. And these old stone walls, cold enough to leech the warmth from my bones. They've got time, and they've got power. And me? I've got squat.

I sit and I wait. On a metal cot bolted to the wall. Completely alone. I wait for Indrid to poke his face in. To say hello. To shove a bug in my head. Something. But nobody comes. Hours bleed by. No clock in here, but I feel them. The ache of them. Night falls. The cool winter sun rises again, low and crooked through a narrow window no bigger than a shoebox.

I lay back, hands folded over my chest like a corpse, and stare at the ceiling. It's cracked and warped, old plaster gone yellow with time. The jagged lines above me remind me of lightning. The kind that dances around my mountain's peak when the storm's breathing heavy. My mind drifts and slowly, the ceiling fades. I watch clouds blow across a red sky.

Tap. Tap. Tap. A knuckle raps against the iron bars. I brace myself for the worst. With a groan and a grunt, I sit up slow, steady, and deliberate. I don't look at the bars, not yet. I flex the fingers in my bad arm. Each muscle and tendon lights up like it's on fire, but it works. That's something.

Finally, I turn. A glare already loaded in the chamber, aimed and ready for the monster I know is coming, the Smiling Man, now a petty king of the hollows. But it's not, it's the girl from the dollar store. Her face is pulled tight, grin too wide, too static. Eyes like oil puddles, reflective and empty.

"Hi!" she chirps. "Do you remember me? I'm Linda. We met a while back, I know!"

Chipper. Too chipper. I don't say a word. Just stare. Waiting for the attack.

"Your grampy thought maybe this would go better with a different face," she says, smile still stretched too wide. "Said you two got off on the wrong foot. He'd like to try again."

Murdering whole towns might do that. Sending monsters after kids, cryptids, and anyone breathing. Yeah, that might've been the wrong foot.

"He wants to bring you into the fold," she continues, like she's offering a sales pitch. "Wants you to see the bigger picture. Be part of the family business."

"Yeah?" I ask, voice flat. "And what about you? What did you want?"

She tilts her head like a curious bird. "Me? Oh, I was tired of my life. Sure, I panicked when they came for me. Who wouldn't? But it's better now. So much better. I have a purpose. A mission. A reason for being."

"So not just a zombie," I mutter. "But a zombie cultist." I nod once, slow and tired. "Great, good for you."

"Listen," she says, her voice gentle like she's trying to level with me. "I think I get what you think is happenin'. That what we're doing—it's terrible. Evil, even. I get that," she shrugs like it's a minor misunderstanding. Like I've just misread a menu. "It's hard to see the bigger picture at first. Those towns, those people? They weren't really living. Just waiting to die. We gave them something back. Gave them purpose. Peace. Made 'em happy."

"Why does he want the Thunderbird?" I ask.

She hesitates, just for a breath, but it's there.

"Like me... like the rest of us... he was a split soul," she says. "A corpse waiting to die. His soul seed came to him from the other world."

"Soul seed?" I raise an eyebrow. "That what you call the cockroach crawling around in your skull?"

She continues, faintly. "He says when he was just a man, only half a being, he made mistakes. Terrible ones. Decisions that caused a lot of pain."

"And now that he's 'whole'?" I ask, already hating the answer.

"Now he wants to erase that suffering. He wants to make a world without it. A new world. One where we won't hurt anyone. One where no one can hurt us."

"I hear Utah's nice," I mutter.

She doesn't laugh. Just stares past me like she's seeing a future I want no part of.

"The Thunderbird," she says, reverent now, "can take us there. It can take us back home, back to heaven."

I meet her gaze, flat and cold.

"If you want to go to heaven," I say, "just open the cell."

"...I know I'm not going to be the one to convince you," she says, head tilting just slightly, like a curious dog trying to understand thunder. "Carlisle, I'm going to open the door because I want to show you something. Something that might change your mind."

Her smile doesn't waver. Just stretches.

"If you promise to behave," she adds, "I can take you."

I stare at her for a long second letting the silence breathe, "...And if I don't?"

"Well," she says, like it's nothing at all, "you can stay here and starve. Or, if you make a run for it, the cops'll shoot you down."

She leans in slightly, like she's letting me in on a secret, "either way, you end up one of us. But it's really important to Indrid that you make the choice."

I sigh and push myself to my feet, slow and stiff. My body protests, but I'm upright. "Sounds like we're going on a field trip," I mutter.

Linda's smile never flickers. She pulls a ring of keys from her pocket and slides one into the rusted lock. The bolt clicks with a sound too loud for the silence. The cell door groans open. I step forward but keep my distance, watching her every move. Without a weapon, I doubt I could take her, let alone whatever's left of this town. And yet, I walk out anyway. Because if I'm going to fall into hell, I'd rather walk in with my eyes open.

She leads me out into the cold morning air. The town's quiet, not the good kind. Too still. Too clean. Like a movie set waiting for action to start. We step out onto the main drag. I scan without turning my head, taking in every angle. No sign of the truck. I clock the alleys, the side streets, the little stream that cuts through town behind the hardware store. It's not frozen over. Still open. Running.

Temptation coils in my gut. I could bolt, make for the creek, dive into the woods, vanish. But they're not worried. That tells me there might not be a way out. She walks ahead like she's giving a tour. Like none of this is strange. Like I'm not being marched through town toward my execution. Linda turns toward me and guides me into Donna's Diner. Well, at least I'll get some coffee.

Chapter 34
Family Reunion

I walk into the narrow diner. Same flickering lights. Same cracked tiles. Still smells like scorched grease and broken dreams. Soda fountain's still out of service, of course. No sign of Donna. I can't picture that woman with a smile, anyhow. Two figures sit in the far booth, backs to the door. A man and woman, shoulders too square and posture too stiff.

Linda guides me straight to them like we're friends meeting up for brunch. She slides in beside me uninvited, pinning me to the wall with that grin and lavender perfume. I finally meet their eyes. They stare and they smile and I don't. I don't know how... to do this. No. No, I can't do this. My chest tightens. My stomach turns. I reel back, breath hitching, vision tunneling.

"No!" I scream ugly and hoarse, full of something I can't swallow. The woman reaches out, slow and gentle, and places her hand on mine. Instinct jerks it away like I've touched a burner. She doesn't flinch.

"Oh, how I've missed you," she says, her voice soft like a lullaby left out in the rain.

"Son," the man adds, his smile never faltering. "It's good to see you. You're all grown up. My, how time flies."

My gut turns to ice. Every inch of my skin crawls. I try to pull away, but Linda presses in, pinning me with the kind of strength that doesn't belong in a girl her size, or anyone breathing.

"It's okay, It's okay, take your time. Remember to breathe." The thing that used to be my mother says it sweet, like she used to when I'd skin my knees or wake screaming from dreams too close to true.

Deep breath, hold it. Let it out slow. The words wrap around me like a comfortable noose, but there's no breath to take, just the roar of blood and rage in my ears. I'm going to burn this world down, this one or the next, if it means Indrid Cold suffers and dies screaming. I'm going to remove his smile if it's the last thing I do.

"Son, you're a grown man now," the corpse that was my father says, easy as Sunday morning. "There's no reason to throw a temper tantrum. We're not here to hurt you. Just want to chat, catch up."

From the carafe, it pours black coffee into the mug before me, like I'm going to forget it's some corpse puppeted by vermin. Steam curls off the chipped ceramic like everything's normal. Like we're some fractured family at a roadside diner trying to remember what love tastes like. I don't touch the mug. I stare at it. If I look up, if I see their faces again, I don't know if I'll scream, cry, or try to kill them with a spoon... and I don't know which one would hurt more. The thing that was my father keeps talking. I don't know about what or for how long. His mouth moves, voice rolling on like static, like someone twisting the dial on a busted old radio. I'm not listening. Not sure I could if I wanted. I'm breathing again. Low and slow. Blowing air into my chest like it might fill up all the cracks. I learned to survive without them, buried that grief a long time ago. Gave it a headstone in my gut and left it there to rot. Didn't need them then. Don't now. These things, they ain't them. They're just another mark, wearing their faces. I hate them, every atom of them and I'll use them. I take a sip of the swill that calls itself coffee. It's bitter and burnt. Tastes like soot and betrayal, but I drink it. I force myself to swallow it down, even as bile claws its way up the back of my throat.

"Okay," I say at last. My voice isn't mine, it's something colder. "Let's talk."

And I give them my best smile. Something stretched. Something awful. Something they'll recognize. A monster wearing my face.

Chapter 35
The Grinning Man

The things wearing my parents' faces drone on, spouting doctrine, mission-speak. Their "great purpose." Their "ascension." How they'll end suffering across all the realms. I imagine lighting them on fire. Watching those perverted carcasses burn. My mom's mission was to raise me. Maybe some siblings who never got a turn. Dad wanted to fix up the old company town. Turn the mountain into a ski resort, make something decent out of the ruin.

These things, they've got their memories. Their voices. But they ain't them. Whatever's left behind those black eyes, if anything, is likely screaming for mercy. Rabid dogs don't get second chances. They get put down.

The three of them walk me out of the diner and down the main drag. I play along—mask on, smile tight—while tagging every alley, every side street. Every door that might still swing open. Every chance to run.

There's a few folks out. Getting on with their morning. Mailboxes. Coffee. Gas station smokes. No smiles. No one's screaming. No one's running. The town isn't overrun. Not yet. But it's started and they don't even know it. We arrive at the town's community center, the War Memorial building. It used to be locked up tight. Now the front doors swing freely—welcoming, like a trap with teeth too far back to see. Inside, the first floor is dim, morning light straining through shuttered windows. A full platoon of smiles stands in formation. Unmoving and silent. He finally got his perfect workforce, unblinking and uncomplaining. They guide me up the stairs. Second floor. I spot a narrow hallway off to the landing, too far to jump without snapping something important. Still... I clock it.

They push open the ballroom doors. Used to be a place for weddings and town meetings. Now it's a mausoleum. Another platoon stands inside, still as mannequins, all rictus and rot. Cheap dollar-store knockoffs compared to the one at their head. The Smiling Man himself, Indrid Cold.

He sits behind a grand old desk set dead center of the ballroom, like a king holding court in the ruins of some forgotten empire. Beside him sits a young blonde woman. Pretty, when tears aren't cutting fresh streaks through the grime on her cheeks. Goddamn it, how did they find her? The mayor had her name. Fuck.

"Good morning, Carlisle," Indrid says, all chipper charm like we're old drinking buddies. His voice bounces off the high ceiling, too loud for the quiet room.

"Did you enjoy your little reunion? Are you ready to rejoin the family? Does the prodigal son return to the fold?"

I step forward. Hands loose at my sides. Heart pounding slow and heavy.

"It sounds wonderful and all," I say, drawing the words out like I'm considering a business offer. "Truth is, I've been a little strapped for cash lately. Family business might be just what I need."

I stop. Gesture toward Bex. Her jaw clenched now. Shoulders squared. She's bracing for something.

"Except I'm wondering why my friend here is present... and so goddamn distraught."

"I sent someone to fetch your girlfriend for you," Indrid says, grin as wide as ever. "Call it a signing bonus."

"Well, that's mighty thoughtful of you," I reply, all smiles like I'm working a mark at the bar. "So how 'bout this—you let her go, send her back to her life, and I'll sign on the dotted line."

Indrid's grin doesn't budge. Doesn't even flicker.

"We've danced that dance before, haven't we, Carlisle?" he says, the sweetness in his tone souring at the edges.

"She stays. Until you've properly rejoined the family. Then, and only then, do you get to decide: set her free... or keep her."

He lifts his shirt with theatrical flair. Two hellish insects—thick-bodied, twitching, the size of rats—crawl from the hollow of his ribcage and scurry up his outstretched arm. Their legs click against his skin like teeth chattering in the cold. My stomach turns, but I don't blink.

"This is all startin' to feel like a shotgun weddin'," I scoff, forcing a grin I don't feel. My eyes scan the room—quick, sharp, and desperate. My clenched fist sparks fire down my arm, old damage screaming new pain. No weapons. Not a damn thing. Exit one: the front doors. Big double set. Big drop. Straight down to concrete and a welcoming committee of hollow-eyed freaks. Exit two: back stairs, narrow and iron, lead down to the street. Safer, if not for the platoon of bugmen stacked like cordwood between me and the door.

I shift my weight. Try not to show the panic prickling under my skin. There's no way out. No clean escape. Three hollows behind. Fifty more in front. Fifty more below. And Bex, right in the middle of it all. Tears dried, but her eyes are glass.

"Before we do this," I say loud enough for the room, "I'd like a moment with the lady."

Indrid grins like he's already won. "By all means."

He gestures, and Bex rushes into me. We lock into each other. Her hair smells like wildflowers.

"I'm out of ideas," I whisper. "You got anything?"

She doesn't speak. Just kisses me. Slow. Deep. Startling at first, then real. Her body presses into mine. Her hands slide up my chest and I feel it. Something hard, tucked in her palm. Pressing through the folds of my hoodie. I meet her fingers. Grip the cold and familiar object. Heavy in the hand.

Good girl. A gift. A gamble. A last shot in the dark. Indrid's voice slithers across the ballroom, syrupy-sweet and smug:

"Yes, yes... you've had your little moment. Now, Carlisle, its time to take your medicine."

Two hatchlings twitch across his face, hungry for purpose. Bex steps back, face unreadable. But her eyes flick to mine, just long enough. The weapon rests snug against my ribs. No sudden moves. Not yet. Let him smile. Let him believe, just one more second.

Chapter 36
The Sorrow That Binds

Not-Linda pulls Bex away from me with gentle hands.
Surrounded by garish grins, we are the only ones frowning. I stride
toward my inevitable fate. Each footstep groans against the old wood
floor. The crowd parts like a wound. I slip a hand into my hoodie.
Fingers find the grip of the dull-bladed weapon tucked there.

My Excalibur? No, this is Nothung. The dragon-slaying sword
of myth. A blade born not for kings, but for vengeance. My not-
parents follow close behind. Slow. Certain. Like death has me on a
leash. The smell of Bex clings to me. The taste of her still on my lips.
Proof that there's still something good in this world, something not
yet ruined... and I won't let it be.

As I approach, I'm that boy again—hiding in the tall grass,
watching a monster tear my mother apart. Watching my father die
trying to stop it. Indrid tilts his head slightly, his grin unchanged.
Wide and unnatural. Not a smile. Teeth bared like a wild animal
sizing up its kill. Two insect-things writhe in the hollow of his
collarbone, skittering over skin and bone and over the darkness of his
recessed eyes.

And still, somehow, a small glint of light still finds a way out of
their darkness.

"Now, my grandson," Indrid says, voice low and dripping with
promise. "Take my hand... and join us."

The things puppeting my parents' corpses step up behind me, close enough to touch. Close enough to smell. Their presence is both a nudge and a threat, encouragement with a knife behind it. I keep my eyes on the grinning devil across the desk. In my good hand, I finger the hidden object, cool and waiting. I squeeze the handle, willing it to fuse to me, to become part of me. The only part that matters now. Then, slow and deliberate, I lift my bad arm. The one full of fire and sparks and every scar he's ever earned me. I reach it out over the desk. He smiles wider still. Reaches back.

A fat, twitching insect creeps across his long, narrow fingertips like it knows it's about to be crowned. My vision narrows. The world bleeds away to shades of black and red, every edge rimmed in rage. My outstretched hand clamps down on Indrid's narrow, papery bones. Fire surges up my arm, through my spine, out the top of my skull. And just like that, my weapon is free.

Nothung, drawn from its cotton sheath. A flathead screwdriver, long and heavy. Epoxy handle worn smooth with time. The most precious gift I've ever received. With one mighty yank, I pull the smiling monster across the desk.

He hits wood flat on his back, sunny-side up. I don't hesitate. I drive the blade down hard. The first strike rips his cheek wide, black blood oozes out like oil from a cracked seal. I strike again.

His teeth scatter like chalk across the desk, clattering against the floor. I can't hear myself screaming. Only the roar, the pounding surf of fury in my ears. Again. And again. I drive Nothung down, guided, precise, into the creature's eye. The socket caves with a sickening crunch. Black ichor sprays across the desk, my hands, the floor. He writhes. But I don't stop. He took everything from me. Now I'm about return the favor. Arms are around me now—gripping and dragging. Little feet scurry up the bare skin of my back. No, just one more.

I swing wide. Miss. The screwdriver punches into the desk with a violent crack, splinters fly. I tear a chunk of the old wood free, but it's too late. Indrid is already up. Black ichor drips from the gash in his face. His grin's chipped and jagged, half a mouth of ruined teeth. They pull me down. Face-first into the floor. Hands, their hands, my not-parents pinning me in place. Holding me for what comes next. Something crawls up the back of my neck. Sharp legs clicking. Cold and wet. The crustacean is at the base of my skull.

Biting. Cutting. Digging. Behind my mother's mask, I catch a glimpse. Bex is thrashing, held tight by Linda's reanimated corpse. She sees me. I see her. I flick my wrist, just enough to send the screwdriver tumbling. It clatters to the wood. Rolls and stops. The thing burrows into me. Its mandibles scrape bone and I scream.

"Get out!" I scream at the bug, at Bex, at the world.

Bex crashes to the floor beneath Linda's corpse, hands scrambling in the dark. She finds it, Nothung. She grips it and drives the flathead into Linda's temple with a wet crunch that echoes off the walls. The corpse topples. Bex straddles it, face twisted in horror and fury, and wrenches the blade free with a sickening tug.

The world's drowned in the sound of scraping teeth on bone, the thing at my neck gnawing through flesh, biting into the base of my skull like it's mining for something sacred. Bex surges forward, kicks my mother's corpse with everything she's got, and I feel the weight shift.

My good hand is free. But my ruined arm, still locked under the grip of the thing wearing my father's face. Indrid steps from the shadows like a phantom, his skeletal fingers clamping around Bex's neck. He lifts her off the ground, effortless. Her boots kick inches above the floor, his grip crushing the soft line of her throat.

Her eyes go wide. She gasps, but no sound escapes. I rip the cockroach from the base of my skull, screaming as it tears free. My nerves howl. My vision blurs. I slam it down and smash its twitching body into the splintered wood floor until it's nothing but black pulp and stink. Fire tears through me as I rise. My muscles burn and blood boils. I turn and shove the thing wearing my father's face to the ground like a sack of rotten meat. And without a second thought I bring my boot down hard. Bone splits. The skull collapses inward with a wet crack. No more pretending. No more puppets. I'm bleeding from the base of my skull. The warmth of it slicks my neck. My legs buckle, and my bones feel hollow. I'm barely upright, ragged and trembling.

Across the room, Indrid has Bex by the throat. Her feet dangle. Her face is turning red, then purple. Her nails scratch at his forearm, useless against skin that doesn't feel pain. The screwdriver lies on the floor between us. Waiting. Poised like it knows what it was made for. There were two bugs. One is dead, smeared into woodgrain. The other still lives. It crawls out of Indrid's ribcage like a prize, glistening black and wet with promise. Then, before I can blink, it's on her. It skitters across Bex's cheek, legs tapping against her skin, antennae brushing her lips. She doesn't scream. She just stares at me, with terrified and pleading eyes.

"All you had to do was, what you were told," says the broken smile, voice slick with condescension.

I stare at him, defiant through the blood in my eyes. "So you're gonna have your scabs tear us apart, is that it?" I motion toward the silent army of smiling husks, lined up like mannequins waiting for orders.

Indrid shakes his head, almost pitying. "They have a different purpose." He lowers Bex, lets her toes touch the ground, barely, then turns to me like he's correcting a stubborn child.

"Corpses don't have memories, Carlisle, but the living do. That's why I've tried to keep you alive, but honestly? I'm getting tired of this game. I've invested a lot into taking you intact... and that investment just isn't paying off, is it?" He sighs with a shrug, "We're edging into sunk-cost territory."

"You killed my folks," I snap, confused and boiling. "They had memories."

"I brought them close enough," he says, "but the truth? They chose, they wanted to live. I offered them that, and they took it. They didn't choose you, Carlisle."

Indrid steps closer. The second insect skitters across Bex's cheek.

"They chose me," he says, voice cold and absolute.

But then, a sound. Wet. Subtle. Like a sponge dragged across stone. Indrid doesn't notice. Neither does the army of smiles, still frozen in rictus devotion, but I do. In the chaos, between the screams, the blood, the fury, I hear it. Squonk.

He's been lurking in the shadows, waiting for the moment. He must've poured himself in through a shattered window, slid like ink across the floorboards. And now? Now he's here. Low and quiet, a squonk-shaped shadow creeping beneath the desk. Coiling. Poised. Waiting for the cue. Waiting for me. I stomp my boot and a warm rush coils up my leg, spills over my arm.

Nothung is in my hand. Squonk has returned. The fluid surges forward like a fireman's hose, flooding across the floor, blasting into

Indrid and Bex. The smiling man staggers. Bex is thrown clear.
Squonk's body reforms in a glistening heap on the wood,
membranes reknitting, limbs re-cohering with a wet, shuddering
plop.

But then, his eyes. Black. His little face twists, convulses. Not in
pain, but possession. The black bug is visible inside him. Fear
punches through my chest like a spike.

"No," I whisper. Then I shout, "Squonk!"

I drop to my knees and pull him into my arms. His skin is slick,
trembling.

"Squonk! Hey, buddy! Stay with me!"

I shake him like I can knock the darkness loose. Bex is crawling
to us. Her lip is split. Her hands bloodied. But she's coming. She's
with us. Then, Indrid screams. A real scream. No grin. No words.
Just a broken thing wailing as black tears gush from the hollow of his
sockets. Squonk is still in my arms, but something of him is no
longer there. It's in Indrid now.

The Smiling Man collapses, fingers claw at the floor and from his
mouth spills a sound. A moan. Deep and old. Not human. Then,
thud. All around us. Dozens of bodies hit the ground. The entire
room shudders with the weight of a hundred corpses collapsing at
once, smiles vanishing like fog in the sun. A death rattle echoes across
the rafters.

And in its wake, the building weeps black tears. Dripping from
the eyes, the mouths of every fallen puppet. Squonk trembles in my
arms. And for the first time in all the long years I've known him, he
doesn't cry out. He doesn't whimper. Bex and I cradle Squonk
between us, watching the horror unfold.

I press my lips to her temple. "Come on."

We move. I guide her out of the ballroom, Squonk heavy and quivering in my arms.

"Run," I bark, voice cracked and raw. "Go!"

She sprints and I follow on failing legs, lungs burning, lugging the bulbous, corrupted water balloon that used to be my best friend. We hit the street in minutes. The bank looms ahead, and there it is, the truck. Untouched and waiting. Bex flings the passenger door open and scrambles in. I rush around back, drop the tailgate, and haul Squonk up into the bed. The creature sloshes, thick and unstable, barely holding form.

"What are you doing?!" Bex shouts from the cab, panic cracking her voice.

"Squonk," I say, leaning in. "Look at me. Please, buddy, look at me."

His eyes are fading. Dimming. Blackening like spent coal. I reach into the cab, rip the rearview mirror free, and crouch beside him. I hold it up and angle it just right. His twisted, corrupted face stares back at itself, bouncing in reflection. That impossible smile, stretched too wide, begins to twitch. Then tremble. Then, break. A low moan spills out, mournful and wrong. Tears burst from his sockets, spraying like a garden hose on full blast. His body shudders, shivers, and melts. Skin and shape dissolve into a puddle, all shimmer and sadness, sloshing over the ridges of the tailgate.

Left behind, twitching in the muck, is the bug. The last one. Its tendrils slither out, groping for something to claim: nerves, veins, a spine to hollow and wear. All it finds is steel. I bring Nothung down with every ounce of grief and hatred I have left. The blade punches through the insect's back. It writhes. Spasms and then stops.

"Squonk!" I shout into the puddle. "Pull yourself together, we have to go!"

Nothing answers but the drip of black fluid slipping down the tailgate. I don't have my rucksack. No vessel. No time. I sprint to the driver's side, yank the door open, and grab the bag that once held my rifle. It's stiff with blood and cordite, but it'll have to do. Back at the tailgate, I drop to my knees and scoop him up—arms shoving the viscous mess, swishing him into the canvas. Thick now, like overcooked syrup heavy with grief.

In one smooth motion, the tailgate slams shut. The bag slumps between Bex and me—warm, pulsing faintly, slowly hardening like some setting gelatin. I throw the truck into gear, tires screeching as we tear away out of the town, and out of the nightmare. The wind howls through the cracked window. Bex holds the sloshing bag in her lap, gripping it with concern.

PART 5:
CRACKING SMILES

Chapter 37
Flee from Rats

Bex sits sidled up next to me as I drive north. Squonk sits in her lap, face pressed against the window like nothing happened. Like he didn't just save us, didn't just sacrifice himself, we didn't almost lose everything. I'm wearing a bandage wrapped around my head like the Karate Kid, concealing the bleeding wound in the back of my skull.

Heading north, the border sign says "Welcome." I'm taking her back to school and back to her life.

"Sorry ya got mixed up in all this," I say, eyes on the road.

She rubs the bruises on her neck with a wince. "It'll make one hell of a story."

"I'll get you back," I mutter. "I'll put an end to this."

"Right, but... how?" she asks. "We barely made it out. You can't fight this. Especially, not alone." She pauses. Looks out the window. Then adds, quieter: "They know where I go to school. They could find my home, my parents." I glance at her. She meets my eyes. "I'm not sitting this out," she says. "We'll stop by my dorm. I need to grab something, something I think might help. Then we head back to the mountain. Together." She turns back to the window, resolute. "I've done some digging. There's lore. Warnings. These bugs? They're end-of-days type monsters. I'm okay missing a few classes," she tells the flattening scenery.

I don't argue. I keep driving, hoping she'll change her mind. We arrive at her university. The campus is sprawling, clean, and polished. Tall buildings of stone and glass stretch toward the sky like they've got something to prove. The landscaping's pristine. Manicured. Not a weed in sight. Everywhere I look, people my age, but different. Happy. Whole. Vibrant kids with big eyes and bigger ideas. Protests with hand-painted signs. They believe they can change the world. "Prestigious." I mutter it under my breath like a curse. I feel small here. Out of place and out of my depth. I leave Squonk curled up in the passenger seat with strict instructions. "Three honks if anything weird happens." He squonks softly in agreement, eyes blinking slow and mournful.

She leads the way, walking toward tall glass doors, like a girl stepping out of a war and back into a dream. The sign to her dormitory says, "No men allowed." I enter all the same. We climb the stairs and slip into her room; she shuts the door behind us with a quiet finality. "Roommate's in class," she tells me. The place is small. Girly. Smells like laundry detergent, incense and musty books. Comfortable in the way things are when they've been tended to. Curtains that match the bedding. A cork board full of pinned-up memories. Photos, notes. A full life lived somewhere softer than I know. She starts packing. One bag, then a second.

"How long you plannin' on stayin'?" I ask from the bed, my boots kicked off and my sock split at the toe. She doesn't answer, just rifles through a stack of cracked and flagged books on the desk and slides a few into her sack. I sink deeper into the mattress. It's a twin, I think they call it. Small. I close my eyes. Not asleep, but not ready to be awake either. Not ready to face the fact that we're being chased across state lines by my goddamn zombie family in search of some ancient bird-shaped god.

Her suitcase is half-packed on the floor. Clothes folded with surgical care, like she's trying to impose order on a storm. The silence stretches. I take a long breath, fill my lungs until my bruised ribs ache. I release the air careful and slow, as if any movement might be enough to wake me back to the nightmare that was today. She watches me like she sees it all. Maybe she does.

"You good?" she asks.

"Nope."

She hesitates, then climbs in beside me, careful not to jostle too hard. The bed's too small for two, but we make it work. Our legs tangle naturally, and neither of us bothers to untangle them. Silence settles. The walls are thin as paper. The ticking of her desk clock sounds like a hammer in the quiet.

"You saved me, again," she says, barely above a whisper.

"You started it," I mutter. A beat passes before I lift the arm off my face and look at her. My eyes are bloodshot raw, but soft. Unarmored in a way I've never let her see. "My folks—" I start, but don't finish. She reaches up and brushes the hair off my brow, her fingers catching in the grit, the sweat, the soot of everything we've been through. I flinch, just for a second. Then lean into her touch.

"I'm here," she whispers.

"I know."

She leans forward and kisses the corner of my mouth. I turn to her; the second kiss is slow. Gentle, but desperate, like we both need the distraction. My hand finds her hip, and I hold it like an anchor. She presses into me. Clothes come off not rushed or careless, one by one: her shirt, my belt, her bra, my flannel. The sheets are cold against our skin but we warm them. There's no fireworks or grand declarations, just her mouth against my throat. My rough hands at the small of her back. She guides me into her, steady and sure, holding my face in her hands, keeping me present. I bury my head in her shoulder, and we move together; slow and quiet like we're trying not to wake something just outside the door. Neither of us says a word, not even when it ends. Afterward, she curls into me. I wrap both arms around her and don't let go. For what seems like a long time, we lay there as I listen to her pulse against my ear. Perhaps too long, the door bursts open.

"Beatrix!" her roommate squeals, and immediately slams the door shut without stepping inside. Bex doesn't flinch, just grins. "Well, that'll be quite the scandal," she says, stretching. Her breasts brush close as she leans in and kisses me with a playful smile. "We gotta get out of here before the R.A.'s show up," she adds, already throwing on clothes, alive with the thrill of being caught. All the excitement and haste without the dread is refreshing. I feel... light. Gettin' laid'll do that to a man. Being afraid of whatever an R.A. is, seems comical after everything we've just been through. We dress in a flurry, boots thudding, zippers zipping, buttons missed. I wrestle my flannel on while she peeks out the door. Her roommate's down the hall, either gossiping or ratting us out to the R.A. Could be both.

Bex ducks back in. "Run," she whispers with a grin. I grab her suitcases, one in each hand, and bolt out the door like a fugitive. She's right behind me, her satchel of books thumping against her ass as she speeds down the hallway, hair bouncing, breath light with laughter. She giggles and I smile. A genuine smile, for the first time in what feels like a hundred years.

This place feels so removed from the insanity of my life. Might've been what my folks wanted for me. As we load up in the truck, I step onto the running board and see the black tar staining my boot. A boyhood memory of my father's loving face fills my mind, before the sound of the wet crunch of his skull takes the breath from me. I try and push it aside, but shame washes over me for daring to feel something different.

Chapter 38
A Dark Realization

The warmth of my companions makes the long, winding road back a bit easier, but I always find a way to ruin a good thing. The feeling creeps in somewhere halfway through the drive. At first, it's just a shadow in the rearview. Then it's riding in the back with us. Before long, the thought sits staring at me from the hood. I stay quiet, probably too quiet, until the dam breaks. I grab Yaya's squawk box. "Carl Cool callin' the Big Stink. Big Stink, come in." Just static. "Come in, Big Stink. Big Stink, do you copy?"

His voice crackles through: "Suave Simian here. You're supposed to check in daily, genius."

"Ran into a... hiccup—"

"Hi, Yaya!" Bex cuts in.

"You're with Beatrix?" Yaya sounds half-shocked, half-amused. "What's the plan, you two gonna start a litter?"

"We've got a problem," I say, taking back the comm.

"Go on."

"He knows everything, he's coming."

"What?" Bex and Yaya say in stereo.

"No time to explain, but he knows."

"What is he—?" Yaya blurts.

"Squonk! Squonk, squonk," Squonk squonks.

"My little aspic," he coos. "Glad you're okay."

Bex leans forward. "If he got what he wanted, why would he still come after us? I don't get it. What does the Thunderbird have to do with you?" Her voice carries a frustrated edge, brows drawn tight.

"He wanted to know where it sleeps," I say, "and now... he does."

"Squuuuooonk."

"It's okay, buddy," I murmur. "We've got ya."

Bex turns to me, eyes narrowing. "Wait. Where is it?"

"The summit," I say quietly.

She scoffs, "I think I would've noticed a giant bird belching lightning up there."

I shake my head, "that's the thing, you can't get there from here."

She blinks, "what's that mean?"

"It's on the other side," I say, quieter now, "outta reach and all alone."

Bex leans in a little, "and how do you know this?"

"I seen it," I say.

"You've been to the other... side? Another realm?" she asks, partly amazed and partly expectin' a crock of shit.

"Can't touch it, don't know how. Don't even know if Indrid can, but I damn sure don't wanna find out."

She rummages in her bag and pulls out that battered notebook. Starts flipping through pages like she's trying not to puke. She goes pale, then a little green. Carsick, but too damn stubborn to stop. "I was diggin' into the carrion bugs..." she mutters, squinting at her notes. "Yaya called them Skudagaya."

I glance her way. "Cryptid lore's usually half-truths and tall tales—"

"Says the man who rides around on an invisible wolf the size of a truck."

"It's a dog," I mutter. "The Yow is a dog."

She waves that off. "Squonk melts into a puddle when he cries. Yaya smells of skunk. I'm way past the point of playin' skeptic, Carl. There's stuff in here that matters." She flips to another page. "This book says they can't control anything but small animals..."

"That don't seem to be true, at least anymore."

"And this one says they can only infect the dead. Or the dying, the weak."

"They got no problem makin' entire towns dead or dying," I say.

She turns another page. Eyes scanning fast. "There's some kind of hive mind. You saw it, how they all dropped at once? That wasn't a coincidence."

I nod, slow. Eyes on the road as it twists up the mountain. "Any chance putting buckshot through his temple counts as a viable strategy?"

Bex shrugs. "We could only be so lucky," Bex says, "he said the dead ones were just hollow vessels. It's the living hosts that had agency. Maybe, without the queen bug or whatever's running the show, they all go dormant..."

She looks at me. "What do you think?"

I keep my eyes on the road. "If that's true... if they're a hive, then takin' out Indrid drops the rest?"

She doesn't answer right away, then quietly, "Your mom, she's still..."

My grip tightens on the wheel and the leather creaks. This wasn't the first time I failed to bury my parents right. "One thing at a time," I mutter, more to myself than anyone else.

The mountain rises up ahead.

Chapter 39
A Last Kindness

Back on the mountain, the air feels crisp and clean. Bex jumps from the truck and throws her arms around Yaya. He grunts, caught off guard, then leans down to sniff her like a curious bloodhound. The big buffoon gives me a slow, deliberate thumbs-up. My face flushes red. Bex punches him in the arm with a grin. "Knock it off, fuzzball."

A black sedan I hadn't noticed creeps up the mountain, tires crunching through slick snow. The engine hums low, more growl than purr. Snarly's yowing cuts through the forest then Squonk stiffens at the sound and squirms up into Yaya's arms. Together they slip behind the trailer, out of sight. Bex and I stay put, standing at the edge of the fire circle, waiting.

The car idles ten yards out, headlights cutting yellow grooves through the falling dusk. Then the doors crack open with a heavy groan. Two stiff figures in black suits rise up like corpses uncoiling from a grave. Good Cop and Bad Cop. They round the back of the sedan like they're moving through molasses, slow in the cold of the mountain. Figures.

"You best have my irons in that trunk," I shout, all edge and no patience. They don't answer, as they pop the trunk and pull out two dark bundles.

"Should we be shootin' them... or helpin' them?" Bex asks, halfway serious.

"Neither," I say.

She squints at the suits, "Weren't they at the hospital?"

"Yep."

They move like molasses in January; I suppose it is still January. Eventually, Good Cop makes it to the fire. Bad Cop lugs the gear, drops a full rifle bag in my chair like it's tribute.

"We come bearing gifts," Good Cop says, voice stiff as his suit. They step in close to the fire without asking, warming their hands like this is all normal.

"What's all this then?" I ask, giving 'em a crooked grin. "You want I should find you a nice big rock to sit on or somethin'?"

"We picked up your chatter over the radio," he says, voice low and flat. The fire must be workin', their speech is loosening up, less robotic now. Almost normal, for them anyway. "After we checked into Flatwoods, we've been monitorin' your frequency," Good Cop chimes in. "Kept tabs. Been doin' our own investigation."

"We brought your firearms." Bad Cop says flatly.

"They were in rough shape," Good Cop adds, handing over a black rucksack. "We had them serviced. Cleaned, oiled. Think the techs replaced a few springs—don't quote me, not really my department."

I unzip the bag and pull out my revolver, now nested in a brand-new leather holster. Fine make. Smells like fresh hide and oil.

"You really oughta take better care of your equipment," Bad Cop says sternly, watching me inspect it.

"Keep the bag," Good Cop offers with a touch too much cheer. "Yours looked... ragged."

"Thanks," I mutter, running a hand along the zipper. "It was my dad's, lost it yesterday."

"We waterproofed this one," Bad Cop adds, "for your friend."

"Squonk," I call out and Yaya reappears with our squishy companion, stepping out of the shadows like he was never gone. Still, a hot breath spills across the back of Bad Cop's neck. I hear her growl, low and steady. "Snarly, gentle." I command, "go warm our guests." The growl softens to a snuffing huff. The truck rocks on its suspension with a heavy groan, and a nearby mound of snow flattens under something massive, then hisses as it melts.

The 'men' in black exchange a glance. They sit stiff on the log beside the fire. Snarly settles across their feet like a great shaggy invisible blanket. "Thank you," Good Cop says, voice light with cautious gratitude. "This is much more comfortable." I inspect my old rifle, dad's rifle. It looks damn near new, 'cept for where the wood's worn smooth from years of use.

"Not to sound ungrateful," I mutter, "but we got maybe a hundred zombified freaks marchin' up this mountain lookin' to end the world, and the secret shadow government sends me... a couple of my own guns?"

Bad Cop doesn't flinch, "we filed our report and submitted a request for support. It'll be processed within three to five business days."

Good Cop chimes in, chipper as ever. "We came right away, though."

I nod. "I appreciate it."

He glances at me, then toward the fire. "So, what's the plan?"

Chapter 40
Last Rites

It's dusk now. Yaya and Squonk spent most of the day bumping down old trails in the truck, squonking over one of Yaya's makeshift loudspeakers, rounding up our strays. Mortimer perches atop the trailer, sipping soda pop through an uncurled tongue. No sign of Fanny, who's to say where she's gone. Then the sky darkens, not with night, but with wings. Massive and slow, they blot out the last of the light. For a breathless second, in the hush of twilight, the Snallygaster could be mistaken for Him.

While they were busy building our army, Good Cop, Bad Cop, and I loaded what was left of my childhood playthings onto a mine cart. We rode it down slow, into the smoldering dragon's throat, until even the lizards were choking. At the last switchback, I wrapped a rubber band around the brake lever and let it roll. Watched it sink deeper still. Afterward, I went to visit Miss Sally in her cavern cathedral. She sat still and silent in the dark, queen of the abyss, sovereign of silence. I talked for a while, told her what was coming. Then gave her an old machete I had lying around camp; placing it in her hands felt wrong somehow, like spray-painting an ancient ruin. Defiling the unknowable, but I did it just the same. I told her to, "stay safe."

I load my rifle and revolver slow and deliberate, each round is a prayer for some type of miracle. Extra magazines slide snug into the new pack's pockets, clean and tight. The lizards even threw in a couple speed loaders for the revolver. Thoughtful.

I teach Bex how to handle the shotgun. She struggles with the aim, too much scatter and too little confidence. After a few too many wide shots, I swap the buckshot for birdshot. With everything in place, we gather around the weak fire, breath fogging in the mountain's cold.

Yaya's up on the roof, fiddling with some contraption, beside the soda sipping gargoyle. He hooks his squawk box to the antenna rigged to the trailer roof, wires twisting like vines. "The bugs want one thing, the Thunderbird," Yaya calls down. "We still don't know if they realize it's sittin' on the other side, but this baby right here'll make sure they don't get through anywhere within twenty miles." He gives the antenna a proud smack. Sparks flutter. Mortimer blinks but doesn't flinch. Yaya drops down from the roof with that simian grace, landing beside me like it's nothing. I step up to the fire, take a breath, and start my spiel.

"Y'all are riskin' a lot, for maybe a whole lot more." I let that hang for a beat, eyes drifting from face to face. Cold wind snaps the silence. "Indrid's the primary target. We kill him, the rest should drop. Go for the eyes." I glance at Bex. "Now there ain't no glory in dyin'..." My eyes flick to Yaya's dumb, earnest face. "And if you do, I'll be ribbin' ya for the rest of my days." A few chuckles. Tense ones. "You know your roles. Give 'em hell, then get the hell out. If it all goes sideways, get in the damn cars and drive." I look out across my strange and scrappy rabble with an odd sort of pride. "That's it."

"WHEN things go sideways," Bad Cop says flatly, "and they will, the odds of this not going sideways are statistically poor."

"A few Swiss on a hill are worth a thousand knights in a field.,"
Yaya shoots back, adjusting the squawk box like it's a crown.

"I don't see any Swiss around, do you?" the s's slither off Bad
Cop's tongue.

"In the words of Nathaniel Greene: We fight, get beat, rise, and
fight again... just don't git yerself killed." I cut back in.

"Also, we do have a dragon, that tends to even the odds," Yaya
shrugs. "Ain't the first time I've seen the world teeter. At least this
time... we got a plan."

Chapter 41
Best Laid Plans

Night falls while we wait for movement, for the edge of the woods to ripple, for the wind to shift. But nothing comes. The fire burns low. The others doze in chairs or sit with eyes half-lidded, clutching weapons that feel heavier by the hour. I'm nodding off when Bex whispers, "Are we sure he's even coming?" She barely finishes the question before something shifts. A shadow unsticks itself from the dark, and there he is.

Indrid Cold steps forward, smooth and deliberate. The gouged eye still weeps black. His grin is cracked and crooked. But his voice? Untouched, almost warm.

"Hello, grandson," he says, like this is a family reunion, "your little friend gave me quite the perspective on life. Feeling the world the way he does, drenched in sorrow, in loneliness, in all that broken hope you folks call living—" He tilts his head, eye socket glinting wet in the firelight. "It's only made me more certain of my mission. I'm not here to hurt you, Carlisle; I'm here to stop the hurt."

I whistle, fast and sharp and a blur of motion answers. Snarly crashes into the thin old bastard like a freight train made of teeth. Black fangs tear through mummified flesh, snarls rising like thunder. But Indrid doesn't flinch. With an impossible strength, he lifts the snapping and clawing beast and hurls her off the ridge like an annoyance.

No!

I barely register the groan of suspension before I see it. My rusted out old red truck, pirouettes through the air like divine retribution. It crashes down on top of the demon, metal shrieking as it crumples around him.

Good monkey.

Indrid's pinned at the waist with only one arm free, twitching in fury. I step toward him, cautious and steady. It never goes easy, never goes smooth, but always ends the same. I barely hear Good Cop calling out behind me, but I don't turn. I've got the bastard. I ready my revolver.

"Whatever your plan was, I 'spect it didn't go quite right," I growl, leveling the barrel at his ruined face. "Plumb stupid not to hide behind your horde." I aim for the hollowed-out socket where his eye used to be.

Indrid grins, bloody and wide. "Perhaps... it's stupider not to expect my horde to hide behind you."

My stomach drops. I glance back. Bex, Yaya, Good Cop, Bad Cop, all held at jagged blade-point. Long knives to each throat. Each captor wearing a familiar twisted and stretched face. And my mother, or what's wearin' her, is the one with Bex in her grasp. That's a nice touch.

No sign of Squonk. Snarly's gone over the edge; I'll have to trust she'll find a way back to me.

"That's some show," I say, eyes back on Indrid, jaw tight. "But I'm fairly certain if I put this bullet in your brainpan, the rest of your puppets drop with you."

"All but one," he chuckles, a bubbling sound wet with glee. Then they move. Hollows swarm in around us, a tide of empty smiles and twitching limbs. They rock the truck. Lift it. Start tearing it off their master, piece by piece. I freeze. Every instinct pulls in a different direction. Shoot. Surrender. Run. Scream. None of it feels right; all of it feels wrong. Behind me, another cluster of hollows climbs onto the trailer roof and starts tearing apart Yaya's radio rig, wires pulled like guts from a carcass.

I let out a long tired sigh, "You really are a one-trick pony, huh?"

Indrid, still half-pinned beneath the ruined truck, spits blood and grins. "I use what works." He claws his way upright, limbs bending wrong but functional all the same. "Your squishy little friend showed me where the bird is," he says, voice slick with malice, "but you will be the one to show me how."

The horde finishes with the truck and closes in around me. I holster my revolver, slow and deliberate. Resignation settling in like old dust. From my pocket, I pull a can of pop. Crack the tab. Fzzzzzt.

The hiss of carbonation cuts the tension like a gunshot. Massive wings slice down from the sky, silent and sudden. Darkness falls. Red eyes flash like embers through fog and before I can take a breath, I'm no longer on the ground. Mortimer lifts me with a firm taloned grip as the world falls away.

Chapter 42
Creeping Infestation

A thunderous birdcall echoes across the sky, long and bone-deep. Indrid's head snaps upward. There, above the summit, just below the storm, a massive shadow beats its wings. Snallygaster does her job well. With red eyes gleaming, Mortimer carries me fast and low before dropping me, gentle as wind, onto the far end of the trailer. I land with a grunt behind the hollows tearing apart Yaya's rig.

Indrid turns and most of his horde follows, beginning the climb up the mountain face toward the screeching giant. Cockroaches scaling stone walls toward thunder. He leaves just ten behind. Four hold my friends at blade-point. Three circle the firelight like jackals. Three on top of the trailer too focused on destroying Yaya's pride to notice their doom.

I draw a sharpened railway spike, cruel and clean. Grab the nearest hollow, drag it back, and drive the spike through its skull. No scream to muffle, just thick black blood pooling like oil under moonlight. Mortimer swoops again, talons snatching them mid-task. A long beat later, meat hits stone down in the valley. Three down.

I crawl to the trailer edge, belly flat to the cold metal. Below Bex, Yaya, and the lizardmen, all with a knife to their throats. There's a puddle at Bex's feet, but it isn't piss. Yaya sees me and winks. All four are ready, coiled like springs except Bex. She's frozen, fear in her eyes like a crack in a stained-glass window. Mortimer drops me behind the captors, silent as breath. I ready the spike.

"I told you the plan would go south," Bad Cop mutters with a smirk, the blade still pressed to his throat.

"A bad plan's better than no plan at all," Good Cop replies.

"This was clearly aaalll part of my master plan," Yaya adds, grinning despite the corroded blade against his throat. "We sent most of the bastards on a wild goose chase, and Carl's 'bout to spring into action. Right about... now!"

The four of us break the silence all at once. The two lizards twist free in unison. A flash of movement, fluid and practiced. Judo, maybe. Years of training packed into a few seconds. They slam their captors into the dirt, draw long, thin blades, and finish the job with cold precision. Yaya twists, beats and hurls his captor into the fire like an enormous gorilla. A scream cuts through the night as the corpse begins to burn, filling the air with a foul, greasy stench.

Squonk rushes up Bex's leg like a geyser, coiling around my mother's hollowed arm, engulfing the blade. It jerks back, stumbling. I drive the spike forward, clean and fast, straight into its skull, her skull. I lay the body face down in the muddy slush with a gentleness that surprises me, but everything in me refuses to look at her. Bex drops to her hands and knees, choking, eyes wide. Yaya grabs the wrought iron fire poker and jabs it deep into the writhing hollow in the fire until it stops moving. Just like that, four more enemies down.

The tide begins to turn. Hollow bodies thud down the mountainside, one by one, weak climbers, peeling away like overripe fruit.

I move to Bex and help her to her feet. "There hasn't been enough noise to stir the remaining three," I mutter, "let's keep it that way."

"Four," Yaya corrects, with more adept eyes.

Each falling corpse punctuates our steps. Overhead, Mortimer glides low as a shadow snatching the hidden patrol with a single swoop. Their boots skim my scalp before vanishing into the stars.

"Okay, now three."

Yaya moves in close and crushes a hollow's skull between his palms, like a melon gone soft. Good Cop and Bad Cop don't miss a beat. One wraps the garrote. The other drives the blade home. No sound. No hesitation.

"How long do we actually think we can keep him fooled?" Bex shouts a whisper.

"Long enough; need to get to our stations, like we planned." I murmur.

The scream of the giant serpent erupts and echos across the valley as it rises above the summit and sweeps hollow men off the mountain side. Her gigantic tail slaps and whips across dozens of the bugmen.

"Okay, maybe not."

From down here, I can only imagine Indrid properly pissed off from this ruse. Not every broken bugman that rains off the mountain died on impact. Many have broken and tangled limbs, but the bug inside is somehow still intact. The agents systematically dispatch them as they crawl closer to camp.

I rush Bex toward the trailer, and I strap on the new rucksack and grab the rifle case. I shout for Squonk and I feel a splash against my neck as he hops into the bag. Bex grabs my shotgun.

"We need a boost," I shout to Yaya.

He tosses us casually onto the roof of the trailer. Bex lands on her feet with one hand down. I land on my back with a thud and a grunt. I charge the rifle, and shout to Bex, "Shoot any bug that gets past the camp fire."

I roll on to my belly and take aim with a sandbag as the resting place for my barrel. Through the iron sights, I can't make out much of anything beyond the fire. Yaya, smashes a line of crawling hollowmen and then climbs up onto the trailer with us. He gets to work reassembling his rig. Says it produces 'electro magnetic interference' and radio waves shutting any chance of traversal to the great bird beyond.

I take shot after shot, aiming at the glints of teeth in the darkness. Half Indrid's army is a collapsed heap of twitching rotten meat. The shower of corpses stop and a massive scream erupts from the summit. I just about see whats happening, before I leap to my feet and shove Bex off the trailer roof.

The ground shakes and the sound of tearing wood and metal stops just as quickly as it erupted. The great feathered serpent lies on top of what used to be my trailer. It writhes weakly as tommyknockers cover the great beast like swarms of stabbing ticks. I landed bad, sparks of pain cascade through my arm, seizing my mind. My rifle is gone. I struggle myself into a semi-standing position, babying my mangled arm and shocked at how close I was to being skewered by one of the Snallygaster's great talons.

Where's Bex?

I follow the scaled leather around to the other barbed toes and find her. Bex, pierced with the curved lance of the serpent's claw. I rush and stumble toward her on my knees. She's unconscious. Tears well in me, and before I shout in a graveled voice, Squonk is flowing himself out of my pack and around her wound. I lift myself up and shout, "Yellowtop!" He rushes beside me with concern in his deep set eyes. "On three." I tell him. We both grab a hold of the caber sized claw. "One, Two, THREE!"

With grunts and screams, we pull the claw from Bex's side. As the wound is cleared, Squonk soaks her pooling blood into himself and eases into her wound forming a membrane around her. We shift the gigantic spike down into the ground, and I lift Bex carefully with my one and a half working arms. I hold her close for a moment, before pushing her limp body into Yaya's arms.

"Get her out,' I tell him, "when things go south, you bail. That's the plan."

The black suited reptilians stand in shock staring at the great serpent befell by the swarm of tiny gremlins.

"You need to get out of here, now!" I shout at them.

"Not quite yet," Bad Cop replies barely acknowledging me. The 'men' in black march into the mess of collapsed and torn wood and aluminum that was my home and climb on top of the rounded bulk of the great serpent. Each gremlin busy stabbing long narrow claws into the dragon, gets systematically skewered with the methodical precision of a surgeon.

"Take the truck and get out of here!" I reiterate to the unmoving ape.

"The truck ain't going anywhere..." he gestures to the crushed, crumpled and torn apart mess that was my rusted heap.

"Just go!"

"Yer comin' with," he tells me with a gruff unease. Cradled in his one big fur-lined arm, Bex seems so small. He grabs me by the rucksack, but I slip out of it and rush into the oncoming fray. From the corner of my eye, I see the reptilians being swarmed by the remaining gremlins, while the great serpent slithers free and off the side of the mountain.

Yaya is gone, with Bex and Squonk.

"Good monkey," I tell myself and draw my revolver.

Then it comes. A gust, deep and thunderous, spills down the slope. And with it... a wave. Bodies crash down the rock in a sick, clattering cascade.

Chapter 43
Into the Dragon's Mouth

An avalanche of bodies tumbles down the rock face—limbs flailing, jaws snapping. Atop the mess, Indrid rides the wave like some grinning god of the damned, his broken smile split wide against the darkness. I draw my revolver and charge, boots pounding the frozen earth and heart kicking like a mule. The horde twists and writhes, thin arms clawing, fingers grasping from a tangled snarl of meat and bone. Groans and shrieks echo like a dying choir.

Up above, a sliver of gold breaks the horizon. Morning, I start to bargain with it.

"Just get me to sunrise," I tell myself. "Let the light burn this nightmare away."

I spot him in the mass. His broken mouth, that hollowed-out eye, gliding through the writhing tangle like a shark in surf. Calm, certain and coming straight for me. I cock the hammer and line up the shot. I just need one clean pull, that's all it'll take. One good shot, and this nightmare ends. He's in my sights, the bastard who stole everything. Just one—Grasping fingers seize my legs. Arms wrap around my waist. The dead pulling me down. I fall. The shot cracks wide, a prayer wasted.

I'm pinned, buried under grasping hands and bone-thin arms. He glides across the backs of his puppets like Jesus walking on water, unbothered, untouched. Getting closer, then I hear it.

A low, bone-deep yowl cuts through the sky, ancient and awful. I crane my neck, grinding the back of my skull into mud, slush and rock, to see four enormous paw prints press into the filth before me. Above them, floating, Miss Sally cloaked in nothing but stitched gremlin skins, glimmering like oil in moonlight. Her long black hair flows like ink down her back. One arm outstretched, machete slick with black blood.

For a moment, even Indrid pauses. Head tilted. Grinning still, but... curious. "What in the world are you?" he murmurs. Then Snarly moves, a blur of fury. She leaps with Miss Sally on her back, and the two crash into the horde like judgment made flesh. Invisible tooth and claw. A blind, sweeping blade. The mass is torn apart, flung like kindling. Miss Sally cuts through to me. Her cool fingers find my arm and pull. I'm yanked free gasping, slick with blood and sweat. I raise my revolver and fire into the horde, wild and furious. A few bodies jerk and drop, but most don't even flinch. Indrid remains untouched.

She pulls me free from the throng and slides off the great invisible hound. Her hand finds mine—soft and insistent—she leads me toward the hidden crevice, her secret place. A silent invitation to escape and disappear with her. To where, I don't know. Still, I hesitate. I stop her gently. Wrap her arms in mine.

"You go," I say, quiet but firm, "I've got something I still gotta finish."

I press my forehead to hers for a breath. Then pull away and guide her toward the crevice's shadowed mouth.

"Please, go."

She stares into me without eyes seeing more than this world, before vanishing into the dark; gone like a dream before waking.

Behind me, Indrid hasn't slowed. He walks with that same deliberate gait. His smile cracked and bones exposed, his remaining eye black and gleaming. Snarly continues to rip through what remains of his army, but he pays her no mind. He's coming for me. Unhurried. Certain this is already done. I limp toward the pale promise of the sunrise, each step heavier than the last. He follows, mockingly close. Like a shadow I can't outrun.

"You know, grandson," he says, voice like silk over gravel, "I must admit, I'm impressed. You've put on quite the show. A bit vulgar at times, but undeniably effective."

He lifts his hand, and one of the insects skitters lazily up his long, bony fingers.

"You've thinned my ranks, cost me resources... it will take years to rebuild. But really, what is time to men like us?" He smiles wider, impossibly so.

"Once you accept your place in the family, all this mess, you'll see is just another petty labor dispute."

The blood soaked bandage wrap that once covered the hole in the back of my head hangs heavy and crimson on my shoulders, like a proper redneck.

"Oh, yeah? How'd the last one work out for ya, gran-pappy?" I ask, voice low and mocking.

I reach it, finally. My boots drag and legs scream, but there it is. The smoldering shaft, the dragon's throat. I take one long, ragged breath, then run straight for the smoke, into whatever hell waits for me there.

"Really, boy? This is getting pitiful." His voice follows me, smug and smooth. "I built this mine. I know it better than the back of my hand."

I hear the crunch of gravel behind me, his stride unbothered.

"I spent years crawling through its veins before I ever clawed my way back into the daylight," he drawls, closer now. "There's no escape for you, not down there."

But I'm already at the dragon's yawning mouth, black smoke rising to meet the sun.

"Stop!" the old man creaks out, voice thin and fraying at the edges.

So, he is afraid. Afraid to follow? Maybe he spent too long buried in the dark. Maybe he's just worried I'll suffocate before he gets his prize. I don't care, as long as he follows. I drag my busted arm along the jagged wall, each contact a jolt of white-hot pain—sharp enough to keep me conscious and moving. I shuffle deeper into the black, down the dragon's throat, where the air is thick with brimstone.

Let's end this where it all began.

Chapter 44
An End to Suffering

I keep moving deeper into the mine. Black smoke slithers along the ceiling like an upside-down river. My head starts to pound rhythmically. Each breath tastes like ash. My chest tightens and I keep going. I cough, doubling over, using the shaft walls to hold myself upright. My legs stumble forward like they belong to someone else.

Deeper.

The pain shifts, less a headache now, more a humming behind my eyes. I'm lightheaded and my vision is swimming. Almost there. Indrid walks toward me, calm and professional. Measured steps like the outcome's already carved in stone. That grin, fixed and grotesque. The bad air, or lack of any, doesn't seem to faze him. Not even a little.

It doesn't matter. I scramble onto a crate in front of me. My crate, full of my childhood playthings. The crate stamped U.S. Ordnance. Wartime Surplus.

Today, I brought matches.

His footsteps shuffle behind me, closer now. Steady as a clock winding down.

"All I ever wanted for you," he says, voice smooth as silk on a coffin lid, "was a joyful life. And even now... after everything... I still want to help end your suffering."

I'm swaying, lightheaded. His mouths multiply—two, then four, then more—swimming in front of my blurred eyes like leeches in a jar.

I can't focus, but I can strike a match.

"Where there's life... there's suffering," I rasp, dragging the match head across the crate.

It flares gold and angry.

"All you offer is death."

I wave the flame in front of the blur of smiles.

"So, in a way... I'm offering you the same deal."

His grin falters.

"You'll die here!" he barks, sharp and biting.

Fear.

I smile, "together, like family."

I toss the fizzing match inside the open crate.

The last thing I see before closing my eyes, is that bastard's panic-stricken face, and I'm finally at peace.

I take my final breath.

Chapter 45
The Sea of Souls

I'm falling through a red sky, toward the impossibly vast sea. For once in my life, I'm at peace... but, I suppose it isn't in my life. The wind whips my face, more vivid and real than ever before. The sea of souls is rushing to greet me, but a dark shadow envelops my view. The eagle, as big as God, plummets wrapping its talons around me. Then thunder erupts around me as its vast wings push downward. I'm rushed upward like a stone reversed in time.

I wake in the dark.

Somehow, I know it's the black cathedral. That sound again, water trickling down the wall, whispering into the stream below. I'm naked on the cool uneven stone floor.

"Miss Sally?" I ask my echo.

No answer, but there wouldn't be. I close my eyes to the blackness and see her sitting by the trickling stream, the cloak I made her, folded neatly below where she sits. She washes herself clean of blood and horror.

I approach with cautious steps and sit beside her.

"Miss Sally, " I say voice low and reverent.

She turns to me with a sliver of a smile, then reaches a transparent hand with bone, tendons and ligaments sliding into my own. She rests her head against me and a vision blooms behind my eyes. Something gentle and abstract. Where there once was nothing, something warm and vivid is growing in the silence, a new virgin world, something beautiful. And before I know it, the vision falls away from me, and her with it. I am alone.

With the sound of flowing water, and with the memory of my hands I navigate myself through the narrow shaft. Every inch of me aches as I crawl and climb upward through the winding stone corridor. Toward whatever comes next. I emerge from the stone wall, exposed to the sting of the winter morning's sun. The world has changed. The snowpacks are a muddy battleground. Outside the cave, the ground is littered with hundreds of bodies. Hollows collapsed like cicadas that ran out of time.

The air is still, even the wind seems afraid to speak. Bex, dirty and blood stained, rushes limping toward me with wild desperation. Squonk still adhered to her chest and abdomen like a second skin. She throws herself into me, arms tight and shaking. She buries her face against my chest, sobbing hard.

"I thought you were dead!" she cries, voice cracking through her tears.

I wipe the soot and tangled hair from her face, my thumb brushing a smear of blood from her cheek.

"Hard to kill," I murmur with a tired smile, "like a cockroach."

She pulls back just enough to look at me, then punches me in the shoulder hard. "The mine erupted with a fireball, like dragon's breath. The whole place caved in! How the hell did you—?"

I place my hands on Bex's shoulders and manage a small smile.

"Everything's okay."

I stand naked in her embrace, the chill of the mountain morning softened by her warmth. An invisible, shaggy force shoves Bex and me apart. Snarly, the jealous bitch, shoves her great unseen head into my chest, huffing like she owns me. I keep hold of Bex's hand anyway, grinning as I stumble back a step.

"Put your dangly bits away already!" Yaya hollers from his lawn chair, a self-satisfied smirk plastered across his wide face. Barefoot, I lead Bex to the fire circle, her hand warm in mine. I drop bare-assed into my chair without shame, tugging her down into my lap in one smooth pull. Caught off guard, she gasps then laughs. We're all together again and that feels like enough.

"Well, we're quite the mess," I say with a yawn, "and we need to get Mrs. Bellinghausen to the hospital." I barely register the sound of footsteps behind the fire until the man in the torn, soot-streaked suit steps into the glow. I squint.

Good Cop. Hell, I'd almost forgotten he was here. His once black suit jacket's hanging by threads. Underneath, green scales glint where fabric's torn away. His latex face is half-slid off, twisted awkwardly around his head like a Halloween mask left out in the sun too long. I don't move. Bex's head is tucked under my chin. Squonk gurgles quietly from her breast.

"Where's Bad Cop?" I ask, voice low.

He hesitates, "We were overrun by tommy-knockers. He... saved me. Sacrificed himself."

His eyes, without the sunglasses, look glassy. Too human for what he is. They ain't so cold blooded after all, I think to myself. I nod, slow.

"I'm sorry."

After a long pause, "I need to file a report."

"Just take a seat, none of us are in any state to do anything useful," I tell him, gesturing toward the log across the fire.

He sits on the log stiff and awkward.

"You don't have to wear that getup around here," I tell him.

"It's policy," he replies, smoothing the melting edge of his mask. "Anytime we're topside."

"Suit yerself."

He leans forward, the latex mask twisted around his half-revealed face, green scales catching the firelight.

"It appears we won the day, and your mountain is saved," he says resuming his chipper tone.

"The day is saved, evil is defeated, sure," I gesture vaguely about, "but the mountain is still lost. The tax man'll come sniffing around any day now to take it from me. Tax foreclosure, they call it. Gonna auction it off to the highest bidder, I suspect."

The reptilian goes quiet and looks down at the ground for a long while, before he raises from his seat and looks me in the eye, "I need to file a report."

Chapter 46
A Mountain Lost

It's February, and the tax sale happened quick enough. The sheriff is meant to come kick me off my mountain today. The Dutch folk down the way heard on the rumor mill, it was some fancy billionaire who bought it. They seemed to disapprove of him more than of me and my deviltry.

Bex wanted to be here, but there's some test or whatnot she can't skip. She missed a bit too much school, hanging around the likes of me. I'm a bad influence, I suppose. I doubt her stint in the hospital helped much either.

It seems so absurd, to give it all up after everything, because some damned accountant told a guy with a gun and a tin star to take it from me. Still, I'm tired and I can't risk Ruby Ridging the residents of my preserve. They're all off in the woods somewhere, hiding out while I deal with 'people problems.' I still don't know what I'm going to do with them all.

The sheriff arrives mid-day with a black sedan following. The new owner, I presume. The sheriff talks to the man in the sedan through a rolled down window, then he simply gets back in his truck and leaves. That is odd. After a moment, that seemed longer than it was, an awkward looking man in a black suit and sunglasses exits the vehicle.

Good Cop?

"I need to discuss something with you, Mr. Cold," he says, matter-of-fact. "In my report, I pitched an idea to my superiors. They signed off on it and allocated the budget for the program."

I arch a brow. "What kind of idea?"

"We bought the mountain during the tax sale," he blurts out, "okay, well, we made BLM buy it."

"The Bureau of Land Management?"

"Yup, that's the one! So, here's the deal. Your work shows a general trend of lowering my department's budget. It would be an awful hassle for us to have to take on more work, so I figure, we set this up as a black site. No trespassing, no tourists. Just you and yours doing what you already do. Keep the strange things away from the public. Your debt is erased, your territory's protected. Everybody wins!"

I go quiet, it's a lot to just hand over.

He watches me carefully then continues, "you don't have to be afraid of losing your mountain anymore," he pauses for dramatic effect, "You already did. I'm offering it back with some added perks."

I glance at the heap of scrap that used to be my trailer. "Yeah, and what about living arrangements?"

"We'll build you a cabin. A real one: roof, floor, maybe even plumbing. You'll be a registered ranger, if anyone asks. You'll have legal footing, maybe a salary" he shrugs, "And you'll never have to worry about losing the mountain again."

I realize the weight that I've been carrying all this time. The weight of the mountain on my shoulders since I was just a boy. No more scams, no more hustles. Maybe attend school with Bex? I don't know what it's like to live a real life, one without a millstone around my neck.

I shake my head, tired.

"No interference, no oversight," I pause, "and a hot tub, strictly for... physical therapy purposes," I add with a smirk.

I reach out my hand and he takes it without hesitation.

Deal struck, deal sealed.

Above us, the summit stands calm, and for once, it doesn't ask anything more of me.

CRYPTID CARL CHRONICLES
CONTINUES IN BOOK 2

BLACK WATER

CRYPTIDCARL.COM